Cassidy's
Charm

DiAnn Mills

Heartsong Presents

To my husband Dean,
my very own Mr. Perfection.

It is better to take refuge in the Lord than to trust in man.
PSALM 118:8

A note from the author:
*I love to hear from my readers! You may correspond with me
by writing:* **DiAnn Mills
Author Relations
PO Box 719
Uhrichsville, OH 44683**

ISBN 1-59660-332-9

CASSIDY'S CHARM

All Scripture quotations, unless otherwise indicated, are taken
from the HOLY BIBLE, NEW INTERNATIONAL VERSION®. NIV®.
Copyright © 1973, 1978, 1984 by International Bible Society.
Used by permission of Zondervan Publishing House. All rights
reserved.

All of the characters and events in this book are fictitious. Any
resemblance to actual persons, living or dead, or to actual events
is purely coincidental.

Cover design by Victoria Lisi.

PRINTED IN THE U.S.A.

"And what might that be?" she asked with a coy smile.

"I get to kiss you next New Year's Eve."

"We both win," she replied, snuggling into his embrace.

Carlos bent to kiss her lightly one more time. He only hoped and prayed their New Year's declaration would last forever, but something inside him triggered apprehension.

sixteen

In January, Carlos completed all of his financial aid applications and mailed them with a prayer. He feared his chances of obtaining the crucial funds to attend Harvard were slim. Yet a glimpse of hope burned, like one Christmas when he was a boy and wanted a new bicycle. Back then, he didn't get the bike until he found a job and purchased it.

He had his sights set on a special Valentine's gift for Cassidy, which would cost more than he could afford, so he requested extra hours from Jack. The day before the year's special day for sweethearts, he picked up the surprise at the jeweler's. He'd made reservations at an exclusive restaurant, arranged for roses to be delivered to her boutique, and of course purchased the gift.

On Valentine's night Carlos stood at Cassidy's front door and teetered on his heels—hoping against hope she liked his gift. When she opened the door to greet him, wearing a red, spaghetti-strap dress, he nearly forgot how to speak.

"You look gorgeous," he finally said, giving her a kiss on the cheek. "Sure glad you're with me tonight."

Before they left for dinner, Cassidy produced a humorous card about a porcupine and a skunk attempting a kiss, but neither could get close to the other—taking off from an inside joke they had because of a fragrance Cassidy once wore that had caused him to sneeze. She also gave him a sentimental valentine along with a huge heart-shaped box of mixed chocolates for all of the candy he'd given her. Sometimes he wondered where she put all of the chocolate in her tiny body.

"And here's what I have for you," he said a bit nervously.

He handed her a card and a small black velvet box.

"But you already gave me those beautiful roses and we're going out to dinner."

He loved the way her eyes widened when she talked, the way she became so animated when excited. And always she seemed grateful for the smallest of things.

"It's not much," he said with a shrug and jammed his hands in his pocket. To him, everything about the evening amounted to a big deal, but to a young woman accustomed to fine things, well, he wondered.

She opened the box and her eyes immediately moistened. "Oh, Carlos, this is beautiful." She tilted her head and gazed into his eyes. "You shouldn't have spent so much money, especially with grad school and all."

Her slim fingers picked up the gold chain and let the diamond heart weave through her fingers. "Thank you. Thank you. I am so lucky," she murmured. "Can I wear it?"

"Absolutely," he said, realizing his fears were unfounded and feeling a bit ashamed of himself to have even considered that Cassidy might be shallow.

"Will you fasten it for me?" she asked and handed him the necklace.

Slipping one little chain into another while pressing back on a clasp was harder than he thought, but after the third attempt it fell into place. She modeled it for him then rushed to show Jack and Kristi. With all the fuss, he felt himself redden.

This would never do—Carlos Diaz, the man who intended to run for public office, blushing like a sixteen year old? His reactions only proved what he already understood. Cassidy had to be the one God intended for him to spend the rest of his life with. But how would it all work out? If he received the funding for Harvard, he'd be across the country with little money to commute. Not only would he be away from her, but he'd also have to leave the care of his mother to his brothers and sisters. The University of Texas looked like the best option.

&

Cassidy fingered the diamond heart dangling from her neck. She'd finished writing out the boutique's bills along with phoning her accountant. With March another week away, she needed to compile all the information for tax time. The year's accumulation of receipts set in a series of file folders looked rather disorganized, but she had recorded each transaction into a computer program before stuffing the receipts away. She much preferred visiting with the customers, helping them select their purchases, and keeping up on fashion trends to laboring over boring office chores. But the work did need to get done, and she'd been trying extra hard to stay organized. Rubbing shoulders with Carlos made a definite improvement on her otherwise lax business habits.

She'd seen changes in his perfectionistic behavior, as well. A few weeks ago she'd watched him mix up the otherwise alphabetized collection of CDs in his truck console. And last Sunday morning he'd added creamer to his coffee without the aid of a spoon. His attempt to lead a more laid-back lifestyle might sound funny to someone else, but not to her. The difference showed he cared and felt a need for improvement. In fact, both of them needed to gravitate toward the middle.

Once Carlos had told her they should celebrate their differences. This declaration sounded odd at the time, but now it made sense. Their strengths and weaknesses should be balanced in the other—a complement to their individuality.

If only she could rid herself of the guilt. Carly often e-mailed Scripture passages that dealt with forgiveness and God's perpetual love. Although Carlos didn't make an issue of her inability to forgive herself, his Sunday school classes often reflected her problem. She didn't mind; his concern only intensified her love.

Admittedly she loved this man, and the mere thought caused her to tremble. If she wasn't right for herself, how could she be right for him? This dilemma could be the deciding factor in what happened to their relationship when he entered grad school. Attending Harvard added to his credentials for a promising future, and while at school he'd be exposed to young women working on impressive degrees. Young women with untainted backgrounds who hadn't strayed from society's or God's guidelines.

Cassidy glanced at her watch. *For such a time as this.* She had a full hour before the boutique opened. Carlos had really made an impression on her. She laughed aloud and grabbed her bank envelope—enough time to make a deposit and stop at the bakery for a chocolate-filled donut and a bottle of chocolate milk. She could swing by his office with a couple kolache pastries and some orange juice. The stack of bills and letters caught her attention, and she snatched them up, too. Wow, all of this work done before ten o'clock, but she'd be in bed before ten o'clock to make up for it.

Locking up the store, she was headed for her yellow Bug when she spotted Thelma Myers walking down the opposite side of the street in front of the courthouse. The idea of ignoring the woman sounded pleasant—their every encounter ended in a disaster—but she'd been praying for opportunities to befriend the rude woman.

"Good morning, Mrs. Myers," she said, forcing a smile. The old cliché of a smile breaking her face crossed Cassidy's mind, for Thelma's scowl did not bode well.

The woman turned her head toward the gazebo situated on the left side of the building grounds as though reading the banner advertising the town's May festival for the first time. This celebration hailed itself as one of the oldest German celebrations in the state, and it had been a topic of conversation for the past few Chamber of Commerce meetings.

"Beautiful day, isn't it?" Cassidy asked.

When Thelma failed to respond the second time, Cassidy shook her head and realized this was not the day the woman intended to melt her frosty interior. Some prompting, however, urged her to try one more time.

"Your display window is lovely."

Nothing. Thelma leaned up against the gazebo, and Cassidy turned her attention back to her car, but something caught her eye. She whirled back around and saw the woman fall against the wooden structure. Thelma clutched her chest and slumped to the ground.

Cassidy raced across the street, fear tingling her fingertips. "Mrs. Myers, are you all right?" she called, bending over the collapsed figure.

Thelma opened her eyes through faint slits; her hands crossed over her heart. "Pain," she uttered. "Help me."

Trembling, Cassidy pulled her cell phone from her purse, flipped up the cover, and dialed 911. Several long moments passed before the operator answered. Meanwhile Cassidy stole a glimpse in every direction, looking desperately for someone to help. No one was in sight.

"I've called for emergency," Cassidy said, not certain if the woman heard her or had slipped into unconsciousness. Thelma's face had paled to a ghastly shade of white. Curled on the ground, she looked frail and thin. Always before Cassidy had viewed her as a huge tyrant, not like this.

Lord, I pray for Thelma. She's not doing well at all. Please have someone answer the phone soon.

"911," a crisp voice replied.

"I have a woman here who has collapsed in front of the courthouse. Looks like a possible heart attack."

Thelma gasped, as though fighting for a breath.

"In front of the courthouse?" the voice repeated.

"Yes, please hurry."

"Do not attempt to move her. Do you know CPR?"

"Yes, but it's been a few years since I took the course."

"Okay, Miss. Use your best judgment. The paramedics will arrive shortly. I'll stay on the phone until they do."

Cassidy stared hopelessly at the ill woman who had ceased

moving. A gurgling rose in her throat.

"Help is on the way," she said, sensing panic wrap its paralyzing terror around her. Cassidy wanted to take her hand, but Thelma had balled her fists to her chest. With fear pounding out a warning to her own heart, Cassidy could only pray and glance nervously about for another human to offer assistance. No one appeared. Her gaze fell upon Thelma—no longer pale but ashen.

Oh, Lord, please bring that ambulance, and please don't let her die. We've had our differences, but I never wanted this.

A siren broke the air, its eerie scream piercing the stillness. *Thank You, Father.*

She thanked the 911 operator and slipped her phone back into the side pocket of her purse. When the ambulance arrived, she stepped back and allowed the paramedics to provide medical assistance before transporting Thelma to the hospital.

"Miss, is she your mother?" a young paramedic asked.

Cassidy shook her head. "No, a friend. I have a shop across the street, and I saw her fall."

"Good thing you did," he replied.

"How is she?"

His attention reverted to the other paramedics huddled over Thelma with their equipment. "Right now we need to transport her to the hospital."

"We need to call Archie," the bald driver said as they lifted the gurney into the ambulance. "He's most likely at home about now."

The door slammed shut before Cassidy heard the reply. She assumed Archie was Thelma's husband, or possibly her son. In any event, she felt a need to follow the emergency vehicle and at least be available until a family member arrived.

At the hospital, the paramedics wheeled Thelma past those waiting to see a doctor and through to emergency care. The clanging of doors and equipment making way for the professionals rushing to Thelma's aid intensified Cassidy's alarm.

She'd always assumed Thelma didn't know the Lord because of her stinging remarks. Cassidy shivered, not with the cold temperature of the hospital, but with the realization that Thelma might die without accepting the Lord's salvation.

Her fervent prayers for the woman's life increased, while remembrances of the many times Thelma had slandered Cassidy's name echoed in her mind. The comments had pierced her heart, and at times she'd wondered if they could be true. Sometimes she wished Thelma would fade into some obscure place, never to haunt Cassidy's waking hours again. Then she'd feel the tug of God instructing her to forgive.

Lord, forgive me for not doing more, for not extending more kindness. With all my self-righteous disclaimers about Thelma's rude ways, I never wanted her hurt.

The sterile smell of the hospital assaulted her senses, and Cassidy's stomach churned as she continued to pray for Thelma's healing and the doctor's wisdom in treating her.

Finally she got up from a waiting-room chair and stopped by the front desk in hopes of locating someone who could tell her about Thelma's condition. Unless Cassidy was a family member, however, the receptionist could not reveal any information.

"But the doctors are with her," the kindly woman said.

Glancing at her watch, Cassidy read nine-thirty. A moment later, the double doors swung open, and a tall, lanky man rushed through. Lines creased his forehead and cemented around his eyes.

"Thelma Myers," he blurted. "My name is Archie Myers, and my wife's here."

"Yes, Sir," the receptionist replied. "She's with a team of doctors now. I'll check to see if you can go back there."

He nodded grimly and the woman disappeared.

"Mr. Myers," Cassidy said. "I want you to know I saw Thelma when she collapsed."

His whole body turned in her direction. Cassidy pulled a

business card from her purse and handed it to him.

"Would you call me if there is anything I can do? My business phone and cell phone are printed on there."

He swallowed hard and accepted the card. His every move appeared in slow motion, as though denying reality.

"Thank you," he mumbled, his eyes beginning to cloud.

"I'll call the hospital later for an update on her condition," she said. "And I'll be praying."

"Thelma doesn't believe much in prayer, but I do," he said with a shrug. "Thank you. She needs lots of folks praying."

The receptionist resumed her position at the front desk. "You may go back to your wife, Mr. Myers. A nurse will have papers for you to complete regarding your wife's insurance and care."

"Can I talk to her?" he asked.

The woman tilted her head slightly. "Sir, she's unconscious."

seventeen

Cassidy watched Archie Myers race through the emergency room treatment area. Shoulders bent, he looked beaten before the fight. No doubt, he cared deeply for his wife.

"Do you have any idea how long before there's word about Mrs. Myers's condition?" she asked the receptionist.

"No, Honey, not at all." The woman smiled, warm and sincere.

Cassidy pulled her keys from her purse and thanked her. She'd go back to the shop—and keep praying.

At the boutique, she phoned Carlos and explained what happened with Thelma and asked for his prayers.

"Do you think my calling out to her triggered the heart attack?" she asked, digging her fingernails into her palms.

"No, Honey. If she'd been feeling better, don't you think she would have responded to you by saying something?"

Cassidy took a deep breath and willed her body to cease quivering. "She usually does, but I'm afraid I didn't help any."

"I'm sure she felt the full effects of her illness long before you spoke to her. Probably when she leaned up against the gazebo."

His reasoning calmed her slightly, but her stomach twisted from her fears. "I hope so," she replied. "The idea of making Thelma angry enough to have a heart attack sickens me."

"Put it out of your head, okay? Are you even sure the problem originated with her heart?"

She hesitated. "No, except I heard the paramedics talking with the emergency-room personnel."

He offered to contact their Sunday school class's prayer chain and inform their pastor. She hadn't thought of either action. Shortly before noon, she called the hospital for an update and learned Thelma had been transported to St. David's Medical Center in Austin for emergency surgery.

After work, Carlos stopped by the boutique. They learned Thelma had survived the surgery and now lay in critical condition. Cassidy didn't try to locate Mr. Myers. She felt he had enough on his mind without answering questions from a stranger. Besides, if Thelma regained consciousness and discovered Cassidy had inquired about her health, it might push her into another attack.

"I appreciate your initiating prayer with our class and the pastor," she said to Carlos, leaning against the counter. "And I'm sure Mr. Myers could use the pastor's counsel. From what he indicated, I don't think Thelma has a church home."

"Adversity is what often brings people to their knees," Carlos replied. "I just hate to see it happen."

"I understand the rebellion against God, and it's not pleasant to realize your circumstances are bigger than you."

She yawned and he cupped her cheek in his hand. "My girl's tired," he said. "Shall we pray for Thelma before you go home?"

She agreed and listened to his deep voice. "Heavenly Father, we come to You right now for Thelma Myers. You already know she's in critical condition and needs Your divine touch. We pray for her healing, peace for her family, and a desire for her to learn more about You. In Your precious Son's name, amen."

Later on, when she crawled into bed, still having heard no word about Thelma's condition, Cassidy reflected on her own salvation experience. What a remarkably clean feeling she'd experienced by praying for the Lord Jesus to live in her heart and to ask His forgiveness of her sins. She'd trusted Him for deliverance from the drugs, including alcohol, and He had. He'd forgiven and forgotten, according to the riches of God's grace. How incredibly comforting to know life held meaning and purpose. She wanted the same peace for

Thelma with no worries about the past, only the excitement of a new life.

Suddenly Cassidy felt an invisible hand lift the weight from her shoulders that had been burdening her for the past four years. A miracle! The hand of God had taken away her guilt and shame. Overjoyed, she bolted from the bed, thanking Him and experiencing a joy as wonderful as the day when she'd committed her life to the Lord Jesus.

She had to tell someone or she'd explode. Her family knew of her struggle, and dear Carly had prayed for her daily since Thanksgiving. Flipping on the light, Cassidy pressed the memory key for her sister's apartment at school.

"Hi, Sis," she greeted Carly. "Do I have good news for you."

Carly giggled. "Is this about Carlos?"

"No, Silly. It's about me. Our prayers have been answered; the guilt is gone!" In the next few minutes, Cassidy explained about the day and her miraculous healing. "I want to thank you for your prayers," she continued. "I feel absolutely wonderful."

She heard her sister sniff. "I'm so glad for you. Have you told Mom and Dad?"

"No, you're the first."

"Unfortunately, they're out of the country, but you could e-mail them."

"I will, and would you pray for Thelma? I know you remember her from Thanksgiving."

"Of course. She looked and acted so unhappy that, although I wanted to strangle her for what she said to you, I felt sorry for her. Let me know how she does."

Cassidy agreed and switched on her computer while telling Carly good-bye. Carlos. She must call him. Humming a chorus from church, she punched in his phone number. Excitement soared through her whole body.

"Carlos, I have great news," she said, plopping down onto the bed.

"Thelma?"

"No." She scolded herself for her enthusiasm. "I haven't heard a word about her condition yet. I don't mean to sound selfish, but this is about me. The guilt is gone." She went on to describe what happened. "God is good," she concluded. "He gave me this on a day when life came crashing down around me. I really did blame myself for Thelma's condition."

"This is cause for celebration," he said. "Do you want to meet for breakfast in the morning?"

Cassidy inwardly cringed. Carlos had to be at work by eight, which meant a seven o'clock breakfast and getting out of bed at six. She didn't do well in the mornings, and Carlos knew her dependence upon sleep, but she could try.

"All right. Where do you want to eat? Oh, what about that little café on Washington Street?" She'd eaten at the restaurant once with their Sunday school class.

"Great. I'll see you around seven. Who knows? This new Cassidy may want to get up early every morning."

She laughed. "Don't press your luck."

"Hey," he said seriously after a little more teasing. "I'm very thankful for this."

"Me, too. I feel as peaceful as the day the Lord took control of my heart."

Hanging up the phone, she typed out a message to her parents.

Dear Mom and Dad,
You will never believe what happened! Guess I'd bet-
ter back up first. For over four years, I've been carrying
around this enormous guilt for what I did to you, Carly,
and Uncle Jack. The shame and memories drove me to
think I had to do something to deserve your love and
forgiveness. Now, I know y'all (Oh my, I've been in
Texas too long!) forgave me, just like God did, but I
couldn't forgive myself. When I moved here I believed by
making a success of my boutique, I could somehow earn

*your respect and love. And even when you said all those
wonderful things to me this past Thanksgiving, those old
feelings crept back.*

*But tonight, God took the burden from me. I mean I
felt the weight lifted from my shoulders. So I wanted to
share this with you. I imagine you knew all along that I
hadn't dealt with it as I should, but you can relax. I'm
where I should have been all along. Isn't this awesome?*

*Oh, would you pray for this lady I know? In fact, you
met her at the boutique—Thelma Myers. She had a heart
attack in front of the courthouse today. The hospital here
transported her to an Austin facility where she had
extensive surgery. She's in critical condition, and I don't
believe she knows the Lord.*

> Love,
> Cassidy

She clicked the send button and climbed back into bed.
She'd tell Kristi and Jack in the morning. Cassidy giggled
aloud. Seeing her up so early, they'd think a different type of
miracle had occurred.

With a tired sigh, she realized the release from guilt meant
she didn't have to rely on her shop or anything she might do
to prove her worth. From here until God called her home, she
was a daughter of the King—a princess, royalty. What a
wonderful concept. Her ideals of helping teens lose the
stronghold of drugs now held more merit. The thought
excited her. Her problems in the past could be used to show
troubled teens that they could win the battle.

Once more she thanked God for His deliverance, prayed
for Thelma, and drifted off into blissful sleep.

❧

Carlos's body refused to succumb to sleep. His prayers had
been answered, and in the darkness of his room he wept for
Cassidy's release, for her insurmountable joy, and for the

love swelling in his heart for this zany little woman. What an impact she'd made on his life. Her soft voice and gentle mannerisms touched him where no woman had before. Those blue gray eyes pierced his heart every time he allowed himself to peer into them. Did she have any clue what effect she had on him?

He'd been working hard on his perfectionism. That evening he'd started to clean out his refrigerator but decided to read instead. That amounted to a first. Last week he'd noticed dust on his coffee table and left the apartment without running a cloth over it. Small things, like not lining up his French fries on a plate before eating them, but dipping his fingers into the bag, grease and all. The kind of changes no one might ever notice, but to him, they were monumental. He'd been enslaved by perfectionism, constantly pushing himself until the stress made him irritable. His mother had been right. If he didn't learn to control his perfectionism, he'd be treating an ulcer and taking heart medication. He'd discussed human frailties in Sunday school but couldn't follow his own teachings. Admitting his sin ushered in freedom, just like Cassidy had experienced.

Whatever would he do without her? Did he dare ask her to wait for him while he completed four years of grad school? The request sounded unfair, no matter whether he attended the University of Texas or Harvard. The idea of Cassidy living in Brenham and him off somewhere else settled like midsummer heat. He knew other guys were interested, but out of respect for him, they had kept their distance. How long would that last with him gone?

And he didn't want to think about how his absence might hinder his mother's health.

All things considered, he needed to concentrate on staying closer to home, which meant attending UT. At least he could continue some semblance of a relationship with Cassidy and oversee his mother's care. The school did have excellent credentials, and the driving distance answered all of his problems.

But Harvard. . .attending there gave him the opportunity of seeing how people lived in another part of the country. He wanted a wide scope of understanding and the luxury of meeting people from all walks of life. When he returned to Texas, he would have the wisdom of seeking public policy that would benefit those who elected him. Too often he'd seen small-town politicians lead with small-town ideals. He wanted more for those who believed in him—his best with God's best.

The quandary assaulted him like a swarm of angry wasps. Giving the problem to God sounded easy enough, but he wanted answers now, today, this very minute. Patience must be the backbone of trust.

Lord, the plans You have for my life are vital, but please let Cassidy be a part of them.

As before, he had no immediate answer, and as much as it frustrated him, he had no choice but to wait for God.

❧

Cassidy phoned the hospital from her cell phone as she rocketed into Brenham and learned Thelma's condition had improved to stable. Breathing a prayer of thanks, she tuned the radio to a Tejano station and began to sing along in Spanish. During college, she'd taken four years of the language, and it helped tremendously with her Latino customers and Carlos's family. She had gained a whole new admiration for their music since spending time with Carlos, and over the past weekend, she'd started singing in Spanish with him. She laughed as she remembered his response—surprised and thrilled. Naturally she didn't tell him she'd been practicing for weeks.

Glancing at the speed limit, she immediately released the gas pedal. She'd had a horrible time getting up this morning, and now she was running late. When she'd stumbled down the stairs, Uncle Jack had told her God promised to be with her in the early morning hours, not get out of bed and drive into Brenham for her. At the time, it didn't sound very funny.

Uncle Jack had hugged her close when she told him about her little miracle. Actually, it was a big miracle. God's wonders were always giant size.

She mulled over what to do about Thelma. The woman despised her, and Cassidy still wondered if the heart attack had been her fault. *The next time I'll keep my mouth shut,* she thought. But what could she do now? Flowers would be a nice gesture. Yes, she nodded, she'd order a nice bouquet as soon as she opened the shop—and alert the Chamber of Commerce about Thelma's condition.

Her cell phone rang, interrupting her plans. Archie Myers's voice greeted her.

eighteen

"Miss Frazier?" Mr. Myers asked. He sounded exhausted.

"Yes. How is your wife?"

"Stable. Better than the doctors expected. She had a quadruple bypass." He paused. "She almost didn't make it."

"Lots of people were praying for her."

"I know and I appreciate it, but I have you to thank for being right there when she needed help," he said. His voice weighed with emotion. Poor man. He'd been through a lot.

"I did what anyone would do. She needed medical assistance, and I was there to call 911."

"Miss Frazier, let's not fool ourselves. My wife has treated you like dirt for no reason except she's jealous of your fine shop."

Cassidy didn't know what to say and thought it better to listen—than agree or disagree.

"You don't have to say anything," he continued, "but I intend to let her know who phoned the paramedics."

"Whatever you think is best," Cassidy said. "I'd like to be her friend."

"We'll see," he replied. "She owes you a lot."

She heard children screaming in the background. "Are you at the hospital?"

"No," he replied. "Those are our grandkids. We're raising them after their parents divorced and took off to heaven knows where. I had a neighbor lady all day yesterday looking after them, but then I came home about three this morning."

Realization slowly dawned on her. No wonder Thelma always looked tired and acted cranky. Her days were full before she even got out of bed.

"Is your neighbor taking care of them while Thelma is in the hospital?"

He hesitated. "I've been trying to farm them out when I'm gone."

She heard a child bellow out another scream.

"I've got to go now. The oldest two need to get ready for school, and the youngest wants his breakfast."

"Sure. . . . Thanks for updating me on Thelma, and I'd like to help in some way. Maybe take your grandchildren in the evenings?"

He chuckled. "Wouldn't she get a rise out of that one? I don't know why I'm making jokes at a time like this." He sighed. "Thank you, again, Miss Frazier. If things get wild around here, I might take you up on your offer with the kids."

Cassidy placed her cell phone into the side pocket of her purse. What a shame those children had been abandoned by their parents. Such irresponsibility made her bristle. Archie and Thelma Myers should be enjoying fun times with their grandchildren, not raising them. Now she better understood Thelma's discontent with life. Cassidy had seen her tear into other business owners at Chamber meetings. Often, it looked as though she simply wanted to start an argument. Her gruff mannerisms most likely stemmed from bitterness about her circumstances, and without the Lord, she had no concept of joy or His grace. At her age, she shouldn't have to be mother, run a business, and face heart problems at the same time.

At breakfast, Carlos listened to Cassidy repeat the previous evening's happenings. She chatted nonstop, excited about facing her future free from guilt. She felt alive and happy; then she remembered her conversation with Archie Myers. After telling him what the man had relayed, she had an urge to do something more for the family.

"So, do I offer again to watch the children?" she asked, lifting a mug of creamy hot chocolate to her lips.

"Sounds like he needs help, even if she doesn't want it,"

Carlos replied. "We could watch them together."

"They may be a handful," she said, studying his face. "I heard them screaming all the while we talked."

He shrugged. "Aw, kids always vie for attention when their parents are on the phone."

She saw a smile tug at his lips. The clatter of dishes and morning greetings echoed around them. Breakfast with Carlos was worth getting up early for. "All right. I'll leave a message at the hospital for him to call me." She sat the mug on the table and toyed with the handle. "Did you write your Truman Scholarship essay on peacekeeping methods?" she asked.

He laughed. "No, I had to prepare a policy proposal. Mine was about home ownership for minorities."

"I see," she replied. "How did you go about it?"

He glanced at her oddly. "Are you always this inquisitive in the mornings?"

"No," she replied. "I'm usually asleep."

He shook his head and grinned. "Okay, here goes. I had to identify a problem that fell within the criteria of public policy. I made a proposal including the stumbling blocks as well as facts supporting my recommended action."

"I see. Sounds simple, but I'm sure it wasn't. How many scholarships were awarded?"

"Seventy-seven from around the country."

"So you're one of the elite?" she asked, not being able to hold back the teasing. "Seriously, can I read yours? It sounds interesting."

"Sure, why not?" he replied, then paused. "I am proud of it." He reached across the table for her hand. "Does all this mean you're going to open up to me? Not let all those wild thoughts roll around in your pretty head without talking about them?"

She nibbled on her lip. "I. . .I'm going to try. I've always been a private person, except now with you." She brightened. "You either bring out the best or the worst in me."

"Always the best." He glanced at his watch. "I'm going to be late for work." He grabbed the check before Cassidy could claim it. "I want a kiss," he whispered. "I have a feeling you taste like pancakes and maple syrup."

Cassidy forced a laugh to cover her tumultuous feelings. As much as she wanted to be absolutely truthful about her innermost thoughts, the prospect scared her to death. She wasn't nearly as strong as Carlos, and he saw things from a unique perspective. Most of the time she ignored her misgivings about their relationship and labeled them as simply the differences between men and women. Kristi talked about such distinctions frequently, pointing out that most women used emotional values when making decisions while most men rooted their decisions in logic. That's why God created male and female and ordained a married couple as one. It all made sense when Kristi explained it, but at other times Cassidy had her doubts.

I am a child of God, she told herself. *He'll hold my hand through the best and the worst of times.*

Instantly she remembered the familiar lines from Dickens's *A Tale of Two Cities.* "It was the best of times; it was the worst of times."

Her stomach churned. She'd always run when things got bad in the past. Her throat grew dry. Reality. She had a new freedom in Christ, but a responsibility to be truthful and open in her dealings with others. She didn't know if she was up to such a tall order.

છ

Carlos hung up the phone from talking to Cassidy and sorted the papers on his desk before he left for the day. Oddly enough, after five days Mr. Myers had contacted Cassidy about taking his grandchildren for the evening. The older man planned to meet them at Jack's place with his grandchildren, then head for Austin to visit Thelma.

Knowing how tired Cassidy could be after a busy day at

her shop, Carlos hoped the kids were well behaved. He didn't like the idea of seeing her worn out for a needless cause. She'd offered to keep them at their home, but Mr. Myers said the house needed cleaning.

He shook his head and scolded himself for his callous attitude. Mr. Myers needed help, even if Thelma pitched a fit about it.

Later that day, Carlos took one look at the Myers's grandchildren and he felt his heartstrings tug. Two little dark-haired girls clung to their granddad while he held a baby boy in his arms. They stared at Cassidy and Carlos with quivering lips, obviously frightened to be left with strangers. All three were impeccably dressed in matching red outfits and had been scrubbed spotless. Mr. Myers had even tied the little girls' hair back with red ribbons.

"This is Autumn; she's seven. Summer is six, and Rocky's eleven months," Mr. Myers introduced proudly. "This is Miss Cassidy and her friend Mr. Carlos."

"Please don't leave us Pawpaw," Summer said. Tears brimmed in her green eyes, threatening to overflow. "We could wait in the car while you visit Mamaw. We'll be good."

Mr. Myers bent to the little girl's level and placed her hand into Autumn's, who blinked back her tears. "Your sister will take good care of you. I won't be gone long. This is a grand horse ranch. Miss Cassidy and Mr. Carlos are going to show you all around. Won't that be fun? And I'll pick you up here when it's very dark. In fact, you'll be asleep."

Summer broke from her sister's hold and clung to the man. "You won't get sick too, will you, Pawpaw?"

"No, Darlin', and I'll tell your Mamaw that y'all love and miss her and can't wait for her to come home."

Cassidy marveled at the tenderness in Mr. Myers's tone. She swallowed and bent to the children's level. "Do you like horses?" she asked softly.

"I'm scared of 'em," Autumn said, "but I like to look at

'em." She and her younger sister shared identical features—olive skin, thick, dark brown hair, and huge green eyes.

Carlos joined them while Cassidy gathered up Rocky. "First we need to have supper. I bet you don't like McDonalds."

"I do," Summer said with a shy smile. "It's my favorite."

"Mamaw says it doesn't have veg'bles, but I like it," Autumn added. "Rocky likes the fries."

Carlos reached out to take Autumn's hand. Now, if Mr. Myers could manage to leave without the baby breaking the sound barrier, they'd have a fighting chance. He helped the girls into Cassidy's car and fastened the baby's car seat in place.

Handing Carlos the diaper bag, Mr. Myers shook his hand and whispered, "Thank you for tonight. I hope they'll be good for you. Normally they aren't much trouble at all, but with their mamaw sick, they get afraid she'll leave them like their parents."

"We'll take good care of them," Carlos said. He handed the man a slip of paper. "This has my cell phone number, too, in case you have a problem getting through to Cassidy. I think getting some food in these children will help."

Mr. Myers reached into his pocket for his wallet, but Carlos protested. "I've got this one covered, Mr. Myers."

"Archie," he said. "Call me Archie, and you have no idea how much this means to me."

As expected, Rocky cried the moment his granddad disappeared into his car, but the girls were good about distracting him. Never had Carlos seen three children look so much alike, three clones with dark brown hair and green eyes. He followed them in his truck and hoped Cassidy could handle them in her little Bug.

After cheeseburgers, fries, milk, and a few moments on the playground, Carlos and Cassidy whisked the children off to Jack's Arabian horse ranch. Rocky cried intermittently; he'd eaten very little.

At the stables, Carlos watched Cassidy with the three children. She did remarkably well considering her only exposure to kids was with Walker, occasional church nursery duty, and a few times with his nieces and nephews. She didn't push the girls to touch the horses, but instead explained why they were different from other breeds of horses in a language they understood. Rocky refused to let her put him down, and with Cassidy's little frame, Carlos wondered if she'd wake up the next morning walking lopsided.

When twilight settled about them, Carlos and Cassidy took the three children inside where Kristi had baked chocolate chip cookies. Even Rocky enjoyed the warm cookies and milk. As shadows darkened around them, Autumn and Summer grew more uneasy. The younger girl swiped at tears with the back of her hand and clung to Autumn's hand.

"You know what?" Cassidy said, offering Rocky milk from a sippy-cup. "Your pawpaw packed a complete change of outfits for each one of you. You girls look like you'd love a big bubble bath."

"Lots of bubbles?" Autumn asked, her face brightening.

"Clear up to the top," Cassidy replied. "And they smell like yummy raspberries."

"Tell you what," Carlos said. "Rocky is having so much fun eating cookies in the highchair, how about if I clean up here and then I'll hose him down in the spare bathroom, as long as Kristi doesn't mind."

"Go right ahead," Kristi said with a laugh. "We might stick Walker in with him."

While Cassidy bathed the girls and dressed them in fresh clothes, Carlos cleaned up the kitchen and helped Kristi with Walker. He could nearly burst from pride with his girl. She'd done a tremendous job all evening, although he knew it was taxing. Sometimes, like tonight, she surprised him with her strength—not physical strength, but the kind of grit he admired from strong-minded people. He wondered if she even realized her potential.

"Cassidy is great with kids," Kristi commented. "I don't think I would have had all that patience at her age."

He wiped up the remaining cookie crumbs on the high-chair tray. "Let's face it. She's good at everything she does."

Kristi laughed and turned the dishwasher dial to on. "Spoken like a man in love."

He glanced at his clothes, then behind him. "Does it show?"

Less than an hour later, the three clean children emerged from the upstairs at the same time Kristi produced several storybooks. For the next half hour, Cassidy and Carlos took turns reading. Rocky fell asleep first, and she laid him on her bed with a mound of pillows and blankets on each side to keep him from rolling out. Shortly afterward, the girls began to nod. They were afraid to sleep in a bedroom alone and begged to crawl on opposite ends of the couch with pillows and a blanket.

At last his Cassidy could have a breather. While they sat on the floor, he leaned her head against his shoulder and she drifted off to sleep. He loved the sound of her even breathing and the feel of her tiny body snuggled next to him. Moments like these filled him with fierce emotions for his precious treasure. He didn't care about their youth or the uncertainty of the future; he simply wanted her with him always.

"Now there is a picture of a man in love," Jack whispered.

"Does it show?" Carlos asked, remembering Kristi's earlier teasing. She and Jack must have conspired against him.

"Absolutely, and you wear it well."

Carlos grinned. No point in denying it. He'd been hooked and caught. Might as well fry him up.

Shortly after eleven, headlights flashed in the driveway. Brushing a kiss against Cassidy's temple, he gently nudged her. "Cass, Archie's here."

She nodded and he helped her stand. "I just had the most delightful dream. You and I were riding horses in New York."

"Sounds like a plan to me," he said and lifted her chin. "Are you awake?"

"Yes, I'm fine; I'm awake."

Mr. Myers knocked on the door, and the girls instantly woke, although Carlos couldn't figure out how they had heard the faint sound. Cassidy gathered up the sleeping Rocky while Carlos let Archie inside. In the dim light, Summer flew into her grandfather's arms, filled with excitement over the evening.

"Can we come again?" Summer asked. "We learned about 'rabian horses."

"We don't want to wear out the welcome mat," he said, pressing a kiss against her cheek.

He glanced up at Cassidy and his eyes misted. He blew his nose before he could speak. "Thank you," he managed. "I didn't even worry about them."

"Wonderful. Glad we could help. Carlos helped me, and together we had a great time."

"We took a bath and Cassidy washed our hair," Autumn said, rubbing her eyes. "She dried it, too. And she found our extra toothbrushes, so even our teeth are clean."

He patted Autumn's shoulder. "I need to pay you," he said to Cassidy. "These youngsters are a lot of work and I'm really late."

"No. This is my gift," she replied firmly. "I won't take a cent. We enjoyed them. Really, they were no trouble. How is Thelma doing?"

He combed his fingers through thinning hair and reached for the sleeping baby. "She's doing much better. I told her who had the kids."

"Are you sure that was wise?" Cassidy asked, barely above a whisper. "Considering the circumstances?"

"Oh, she'll get over it, but she wants to see you."

nineteen

Cassidy gulped. She didn't dare say anything derogatory about Thelma in front of her husband and grandchildren. But if Cassidy visited her at the hospital, the woman would have a captive audience. As angry as she'd been in the past, Thelma could either hurl her barbs until Cassidy left the room or work herself into another heart attack. In any event, Cassidy didn't relish the idea of a confrontation.

"Could you visit her tomorrow before you go to work?" Mr. Myers asked. "She's anxious."

I bet, Cassidy thought. "Uh. . .in the morning is fine. How long are visiting hours?" The thought of another early morning suddenly registered.

"Oh, you can stay as long as you want," he replied.

Her mind began to spin, but she refused to allow Mr. Myers or the children to notice her anxiety. Autumn and Summer hugged her and Carlos, and Rocky slept blissfully. She'd rather take care of these precious children full-time than face their grandmother in the morning.

"Do you want me to go with you?" Carlos asked as they waved good-bye. "It's a good hour-and-a-half drive from here."

"Wonderful idea, but she asked to see me not us," Cassidy said, feeling the stress of the past few hours tugging her toward blissful sleep. She peered into his face, and his dark eyes narrowed. "I'll be fine. What can one woman do in a hospital bed while recovering from a quadruple bypass?"

He drew her close to him. She leaned against his chest and heard the pounding of his heart. Someday she might tell him she loved him, but not for a long time—not until he'd decided about grad school and had his future carefully mapped out. By then, he might not care if she loved him or not.

"Your heart is beating a bit fast," she said.

"Only when it's within touching distance of you."

She smiled and savored his embrace. If only life could be this simple. No concerns for children abandoned by their parents. No worries for tired grandpas. No fear of tackling grumpy ladies, and no selfish thoughts about the man she loved.

The following morning found her on the elevator riding up to see Thelma. She'd prayed and sung along to music from a contemporary Christian radio station all the way to Austin, desperately hoping Thelma would be sleeping or sedated. A sweet thought passed through her mind. What if the doctor happened to be in Thelma's room? She'd surely restrain herself in mixed company. Cassidy could even cut the visit short.

When she stepped into the hospital room, no one stood around to interrupt the visit. Between the heart monitor and an IV, the woman looked anything but ferocious. Cassidy had never noticed the many lines etching her face, tired lines indicating stress and discomfort. Thelma opened her eyes when Cassidy approached her, the familiar disgust tightening the woman's features.

"You came," the woman murmured. Her voice came in weak strands, confirming Cassidy's suspicions that death had knocked on the woman's door.

"Yes. Your husband said you wanted to see me."

"Only for a few minutes. I'm very tired."

Cassidy approached the bed. "Are you feeling better?"

She closed her eyes and moistened her lips while Cassidy studied the monitor. "Like warmed over death." For the first time Cassidy viewed a faint smile. Then Thelma sobered. "Why?" the sick woman asked.

"Why what?"

"Why did you help me? I've done nothing but make your life miserable since you opened your boutique." She turned her head on the pillow and her eyelids fluttered.

"You were in pain and needed emergency help," Cassidy said, inching closer to Thelma's side.

"That's not a good answer." She paused, her lips pressed firmly together. "And why did you offer to take the children?"

Cassidy sighed. "I wanted to be of some assistance, especially when I learned your husband was having a difficult time finding care for them."

"They are good children," Thelma said.

"Yes," Cassidy agreed, "precious and loving." She picked up a stack of colored pictures. "I'm sure you cherish these."

Another smile graced Thelma's lips. "When they first came to live with us, I didn't know how we would manage, but it's worked out fine until now." She paused and took a deep breath. "Normally, I see Autumn off to school before going to work. Archie puts Summer on the afternoon kindergarten bus and takes care of Rocky. We have a back-up sitter but rarely use her."

"Anytime I can watch them is fine with me," Cassidy replied. Her hands shook as she realized Thelma truly made her uncomfortable.

Silence followed while Cassidy groped for something to say. She didn't want to ask when Thelma would be released, simply because she'd just volunteered to keep the children. It would make her offer sound insincere.

"Did you want to discuss something with me?" Cassidy finally asked.

Thelma eased back on her pillow and closed her eyes. The color of the bed linens matched the pallor of her skin. "Facing death does some strange things to a person. When my life flashed before my eyes—a cliché, but oh so true—I realized I wasn't pleased with my surly disposition toward a good many people. You included. I'd like to apologize for taking out my personal problems on you and thank you for reaching out to my family."

"It's all right."

Thelma sighed. "I simply don't understand why."

"I'm a Christian," Cassidy replied without hesitation.

"I used to be. Well, guess I still am; I just don't act like it." She turned toward Cassidy. "When I get out of here and on my feet again, I'll be taking the children to church. With the upheaval in their lives, they need to know Jesus loves them."

Cassidy smiled. What had Carlos said about people finding the Lord during adversity? "We have a great church."

"Yes, your pastor came to see me."

Another uncomfortable silence.

"I'd like to tell you about the children's parents," Thelma began. "It doesn't excuse my bad behavior, but it does give a reason for it."

Cassidy pulled up a chair closer to the bed.

Thelma swallowed hard as though summoning strength to talk. "My daughter spent her teen years in and out of trouble. I'm not sure why. Does a parent ever really know, even when they are active in church?" A tear slipped from her eye and slowly trickled down her pale cheek. "Well, when Rachel graduated from high school, she informed us that she was pregnant and the father wanted to marry her. Against our wishes they married. The young man had the same troubled past as she did, and both of them continued with the same lifestyle afterwards." She shook her head as though trying to rid her mind of the unpleasant memories. "Right after Rocky was born, they were arrested for drug possession. Rather than allow the children to go into foster care, we took over. We're trying to make it permanent."

"I'm so sorry," Cassidy murmured.

Thelma glanced out the window and back to her before continuing. "I love those children and I don't ever regret taking them in. Some days I'm so tired, and of course that makes Archie feel badly since he's retired. You see; he's not well either." The lines in her face deepened. "When I saw you—so young and pretty, with such a promising future—

open your boutique, I became jealous. All I could think was that my daughter had had the same opportunities and thrown them away."

Her saddened gaze wrenched Cassidy's heart. Thelma took a labored breath. "The day of the heart attack, I received a letter from Rachel. She'd been in drug rehab and said she wanted to start all over. She asked me if she could come home to live, to be a mother, get a decent job, and start taking classes to better herself. She said she wanted to divorce her husband."

Thelma shook her head and rubbed her dampened cheeks. "I know I'm a hardened old woman, but the idea of subjecting my precious grandbabies to their mother made me sick. The more I thought about it, the more I wanted to protect them." She glanced at Cassidy, her eyes pleading for understanding. "I love my daughter, but she's made such a mess of her life and those children. They are finally sleeping all night, feeling somewhat secure, and eating regular meals. All those things children need to survive. Anyway, that's what led up to the heart attack."

"Does your daughter know?" Cassidy felt the floodgate open and her tears rolled down her cheeks.

"Not yet. She's called the house, but Archie has put her off. I have a friend minding the shop, and Rachel's called there too." She turned toward the window. "I simply don't know what to do. What if she's serious? What if my little ones are going to be hurt again? I couldn't bear to see them go through that again."

"Oh, Mrs. Myers. I don't know what to say, except I had a drug problem when I was in my teens. That's when I found the Lord and realized how much He loved me. Without my family's support, I wouldn't have climbed out of the ugliness and claimed the better life God intended for me."

Thelma studied her intently, and she slipped her hand from beneath the sheet. Cassidy grasped it, her tears still rolling uncontrollably.

"If she comes back, maybe I could talk to her, be a friend," Cassidy said.

"Would you really befriend her?" Thelma asked. She sniffed and closed her eyes. "Cassidy, I'm so sorry for all I've done."

She wanted to hold her, hug her, and cry with her, but she feared the machines would go crazy. Instead, she squeezed her hand. "Does this mean we're friends?" Cassidy asked, attempting a smile while she reached for a tissue.

"You bet," Thelma replied. "You're stuck with this crabby old lady."

Cassidy cried all the way back to Brenham. She thanked God for the miracle that had just taken place and for her new friend. She prayed for Thelma and Archie, the children, and their daughter, Rachel. Overcoming her addiction to drugs and its abusive lifestyle had been tough with the Lord. How much harder for one who didn't know His unconditional love? The entire family needed to communicate, the very thing Cassidy struggled with constantly. Yet, no matter how difficult, they all needed to be transparent if they were to recover from this nightmare.

Thelma had mentioned that her daughter grew up in the church. Maybe the young woman had strayed from God because of her friends.

Cassidy phoned Carlos and cried again.

"Are you crying because you're happy for you and Thelma or sad about the daughter?" he asked.

"Both," she sobbed. "I'm sorry; you must think I'm terribly dramatic."

"Not at all." He chuckled. "I'm glad you're telling me how you feel. Look how far we've come."

❧

March swept into April dotting the countryside with patches of wildflowers and bringing warm temperatures. Cassidy discovered bluebonnets during a Sunday afternoon drive, and Carlos had to stop the car.

"Can I pick them?" she asked excitedly.

He laughed at her enthusiasm and thought how much he wanted to tell her of his love. "You can't, Cass. Bluebonnets are the state flower, and they're protected by law."

Her eyes twinkled, and he knew she had some scatter-brained idea. "Can we dash into town and buy one of those instant cameras? I really would like to send pictures of these flowers to Mom and Carly."

"I figured you'd think along those lines," he replied. "I've got a camera with a full roll of film behind the seat. You snuggle into those bluebonnets, and I'll snap some pictures."

She wrapped her arms around his neck, her eyes sparkling brighter than the sunshine beaming down on them and certainly lovelier than the wildflowers. At that moment he again wanted to tell her how much she meant to him—how much he loved her—but he couldn't. Not yet.

As he focused on his future away from Brenham, she dug deeper into the community. His mother adored her, often claiming she'd trade Carlos in on a new daughter if he didn't behave himself. Archie and Thelma's daughter, Rachel, had moved home, and Cassidy spent hours with her. The two had attended a group therapy session called Celebrate Recovery at an area church, and Cassidy had transported Rachel to the community college in town to register for a summer class. The entire family had started attending church and receiving counseling. From the contented looks on their faces, the wounds in their relationships were on the way to being healed.

The first of May ushered in the balmy breezes of summer and the promises of hot, lazy days. Carlos and Cassidy found time for picnics, horseback riding, and an occasional trip to Austin. Happiness soared through his spirit, and he didn't care if the smile on his face betrayed his heart's secret.

One afternoon, he stopped by his apartment for lunch and checked on the mail. Thumbing through the junk advertise-ments, two envelopes captured his attention, one from

Harvard and one from the source of a possible grant. He'd received notification of a large scholarship the week before, but he hadn't told anyone yet. So much depended on funding. More and more he realized God wanted him to attend Harvard. The rest of the dilemma surrounding his mother and Cassidy would work out for the best. If only he knew what that best looked like.

Habitually he reached for the letter opener and carefully slit the Harvard envelope along one end. With a prayer, he pulled the sheet of paper out and began reading.

He'd been accepted.

Carlos didn't know whether to holler or cry. So much depended on the contents of the other envelope. He could make it fine with the other scholarship money, but an additional grant would allow him to finally reveal his feelings for Cassidy.

He placed the acceptance letter on the counter and stared at the other envelope. Whatever its contents, it set the pace for his immediate future. A part of him didn't want to know at all, preferring waiting and hoping to reading an all too real rejection.

"Coward," he muttered, "where's your faith?"

He rubbed his sweaty palms together and reached for the letter opener. It slipped from his hands to the floor.

Maybe he needed a soda; his throat felt extremely dry. Reaching into the fridge, he pulled out a can and wiped off the top before popping the lid. The cold metal touched his lips, and he drank long and deep while praying for good news. Several minutes later, when the clock indicated he had to open the envelope now or wait until after work, he pulled out the letter.

He digested every word, then trembled, wondering what to do next. The last time he'd received good news, he'd phoned his mother first. This time, however, he needed to call Cassidy. What would be her reaction? They hadn't talked much about it lately, mainly because his heart wanted one grad school and his head desired another.

He'd have to call her on his way to work.

"Cassidy," he said once she answered at the boutique. "Do you have customers?"

"No," she replied. "What's wrong, Carlos? You sound terrible."

twenty

"It's not bad news," Carlos said, but the tone of his voice confused her. "I've been accepted into Harvard."

Cassidy squealed. "Carlos how wonderful! I'm so excited for you. But isn't acceptance a given with the Truman Scholarship?"

"Possibly; it certainly helped." He paused. "Are you really okay with this? Can you handle a boyfriend living on the other side of the country?"

"There's E-mail and the phone," she replied. "Oh, my. . . your mother. What did she say?"

"I haven't told her yet. I wanted you to be the first," he said, his voice hinting of trepidation.

"Why am I more excited than you?" she asked, rummaging through her mind for a clue to his lack of enthusiasm.

"I'm a guy; we don't jump up and down like females."

"Except during sports," she said.

He laughed. "Okay, I'm not believing this thing, yet. You might have to kiss me and see if I turn into a prince or a toad."

"Let me take you out to dinner for a real celebration," she said, nibbling on her lip. "You can let me test out the prince or toad thing." When he hesitated, she added, "My treat. You don't want to take away my generous spirit, do you?"

"All right," he said slowly. "I'll meet you at the shop after work."

"Call your mom," she said with a giggle. "She'll be jumping up and down about the news, too."

Cassidy hung up and took a deep breath. *Well, Girl, you carried that off pretty well.* She shook her head in an effort to dispel the anxiety racing through her veins. God had paved the way for Carlos's success. She should be rejoicing, thanking

148

Him for presenting Carlos with this opportunity. Harvard. One day his résumé would list that fine school as the place where he obtained his law and public policy degree. He'd be touching shoulders with the elite. Sharing classes with intelligent men and women who would one day help lead this country.

She shivered, hating the thoughts pounding in her head. How soon before Carlos met a super-bright woman working on her law degree, a woman whose family dripped with a heritage of old money and politics, a woman who could further his career? Cassidy felt like a country bumpkin from New York. Granted, her family had wealth, but it certainly did not possess political prestige.

I'm a selfish little girl, she scolded. *I'm jealous and I want to be with Carlos.* She could handle a long-distance romance; couples did it all the time. Or did he intend to break it off? And when would she see him? Although he'd been accepted into Harvard and he had the Truman Scholarship, which assisted him with thirty thousand dollars, he'd still have to work. Airfare was expensive, and he'd have to find a free weekend to fly back to Texas. And what about her? She'd need to find someone suitable to mind the shop.

Cassidy paced across the wooden floor of the boutique. Her thoughts refused to be turned off. She feared losing Carlos, plain and simple. When it happened she'd be ready and act like it didn't matter. She'd wish him well and invite him to e-mail from time to time. She could handle it. After all, she should have his best interests at heart—not the self-centered, childish thoughts that busily twisted her heart and stomach.

Lord, help me through this. I want to encourage and support him and push my fears aside. I know what the Bible says about love, and it means to give without thought of reward. I can do this, but only with Your help.

Carlos met her at the shop at five o'clock. He wore his special smile and her favorite blue shirt.

"Would you mind if after dinner we drove by my mother's?"

he asked, taking her hand. "I really am not a mama's boy, but she wanted to congratulate me in person."

"Of course." Cassidy laughed. "I'd like to see her, too."

"She claims she'll have to buy a computer so she can keep up with me through e-mail." A shadow passed over his face.

"Carlos? What's wrong?"

He pulled her close to him. "Just thinking I will have to depend on my brothers and sisters to check in on Mom. I know they're capable—"

"They will do fine," she said, planting a kiss on his dimpled cheek. "And I'll help, too."

He rested his chin on her head and sighed. "I miss you already. This isn't going to be easy."

"Let's not think about our separation right now. We have all summer before you have to leave. I'm starved and we have some celebrating to do."

All during dinner she forced enthusiasm. She hated herself the entire time, but she didn't dare let him see how upset she was at the prospect of him leaving. They did have all summer to adjust to the changes between them, and as soon as she resolved the doubts creating havoc in her mind, she'd be able to talk about it. They'd gone to his favorite restaurant which prepared his steak just the way he liked it, and she insisted he have his favorite New York cheesecake, a joke between them.

"Let's go see your mother," she said once they finished their coffee and dessert. "She's probably called all of your brothers and sisters by now."

"And the neighbors," he added with a laugh. He studied her for a moment. "What's wrong, Cass? You're not yourself."

She feigned surprise. "Nothing, except I'm excited for you."

"Are you sure?"

"Uh-uh," She winked at him. "I'm planning all the e-mails I'm going to send your way this fall."

On the way to his mother's house, she purposefully turned up a Christian radio station and urged him to sing with her. Later, in the darkness of her room, she'd pray and ask God to forgive her immature thoughts. Already she felt better; she could adjust.

When they reached the Diaz home, Carlos's mother beamed with pleasure. She couldn't sit or stand still; instead she walked and talked constantly. While Carlos and Cassidy attempted to calm her down, the phone rang incessantly with well-wishers.

"Isn't this simply wonderful?" Isabella asked, while Carlos talked to his brother. *"Mi hijo,* a Harvard graduate. He will do so well, and who knows? Someday he may be president. Can you imagine? Our Carlos in the White House?"

Cassidy laughed. "President Diaz has a great sound."

Isabella's face darkened, and she shook her head. "Oh, running for any public office will be hard for him."

"Why?" Cassidy asked. "He's brilliant, and everyone loves him. Plus, he loves the Lord."

"I know," the woman said sadly. "But my Pepe, he's in jail. Those politicians like to dig up terrible things about people— the things families are ashamed of." She gazed into Cassidy's face and offered a faint smile. "I'm so glad he has you, a good girl from a good family. You are perfect for my Carlos."

Cassidy felt herself grow pale and feverish at the same time. Pepe's past might ruin Carlos's chances in the political arena, but if his brother's reputation didn't blacken his future, she certainly would. Drugs. The trial throwing Uncle Jack in jail. The rehab.

Why fool herself? God loved and cherished her, but in the world's eyes, she'd destroy Carlos's dreams.

❧

Carlos had detected Cassidy's uneasiness from the moment he stepped into the boutique late that afternoon. How well he knew the challenge of getting her to express her true feelings. She'd come a long way in this area, but from the determined lift of her chin, the chances of finding out what was bothering her tonight looked slim. Yet he must try, or the matter would drive him crazy.

"Cassidy, why don't you tell me what's wrong rather than keep it all bottled up inside?"

She sat leaning against the truck door as though she contemplated taking flight. Silence. He wanted to shout at her when she clammed shut like this, but losing his temper would accomplish nothing.

"I'd like to know what's bothering you."

He could feel her gaze on him, and he took the opportunity to pull off the road. Once stopped, he turned to draw her into his arms, but she resisted.

"I don't think it's a good idea for us to see each other anymore," she said slowly.

"And why have you come to such a ridiculous conclusion?" He maintained a gentle tone, but anger mounted inside him.

"It will make things easier when you move to Boston."

"Where did you get such a stupid idea?"

"It makes perfectly good sense to me, because our lives are going in separate directions. We need to be realistic; we're headed for a disaster."

"That's absolutely idiotic." He realized the sarcasm in his words when she stiffened. "I didn't mean to—"

"See," she said calmly, "already you're frustrated. We'll both end up miserable."

"Haven't the past nine months meant anything to you?"

She turned her attention to the window. "Of course they've been. . .very nice, but all good things must come to an end."

"That's all you have to say? A trite cliché, which I'm sure has wonderful Christian origins."

"Oh, so now you're saying because I feel the logical and responsible thing to do is to go our different ways, I'm not Christian? Thanks, I appreciate your confidence."

"Sounds to me like you aren't disciplined enough to maintain a long-distance relationship," he said. "A local guy got your attention?"

She whirled around to face him. "What a nasty thing to say. I do have your best interests in mind. Think about it, Carlos. Use your head. Aren't you the perfectionist who weighs everything before you make a decision? The problem here is I took the initiative and not you. I've damaged your male ego."

Carlos whipped around and started up the truck. His temper had gotten the best of him, and he'd best keep quiet. He despised himself for bellowing at her like a mad bull, but she'd struck a raw nerve.

All the joy he'd felt earlier in the day dissipated with her declaration. He refused to believe she wanted to end it. Maybe he should have told her about the other grants and scholarships, the ones enabling them to live as husband and wife in Boston. Did she really think he could ever find another woman to replace her? He wanted to tell her he loved her and talk about a life together, but not now. They were both angry and needed to cool down. Why had he considered Harvard at all? Surely he'd misunderstood God's direction.

His thoughts drifted back to dinner. She'd been tense and too excited about the news, but her response could have been merely apprehension about the months ahead. Then something had happened at his mother's. But what? His mother had beamed with enthusiasm. Could she have indirectly said something to Cassidy? He'd call her as soon as he took Cassidy home.

When he reached the driveway to Jack and Kristi's ranch, Cassidy opened the truck door before he had a chance to turn off the engine. She slammed it without a word, and he chose not to say anything either. What good would it do after what they'd said to each other?

Picking up his cell phone, he started to punch in his mother's programmed code but quickly disconnected the call. Running to Mama with his problems made him sound like a kid. Right now he needed to go home and pray. God had the answer.

A gnawing thought bit through his tumultuous emotions, one he failed to accept. He might have just lost Cassidy.

twenty-one

Cassidy bit back the tears until after she'd closed the door of her bedroom. Thankfully, Kristi and Uncle Jack were asleep and she didn't have to face them. Her throat burned from swallowing the emotions threatening to consume her. Repeatedly she told herself she'd done the right thing. The hopes of Carlos's aspirations being realized looked bleak if he were saddled with her past.

Her decision had nothing to do with the burden God had lifted from her, but it had everything to do with the intensity of her feelings for Carlos. Love meant giving up selfish desires for the betterment of others.

Before the Lord took control of her life, she wouldn't have been interested in Carlos or his godly ways. And before she experienced release from the guilt and shame, she'd have already been convinced she was destroying his life. Tonight she desperately wanted him, his life, and his love, but someday he'd grow to regret their relationship, and she couldn't permit apathy to poison their relationship.

Crawling into bed, she wept until she ached. She wanted to pray, but the words refused to come. God understood her heart even if she couldn't voice the pain. Isabelia Diaz had innocently spoken the truth. Much as she wanted to, Cassidy couldn't deny or ignore it.

She recalled earlier in the evening when her selfish thoughts centered on Carlos leaving for Boston and leaving her alone. How trite and immature. Working through those fears now sounded easy, and she could have eventually voiced them in total honesty. They had come a long way when it came to communication, but apparently not far enough. If she'd told him the truth this evening, he would have shrugged it off as though it meant nothing. She could hear him say her conclusions rated somewhere between ridiculous and irrelevant. The finality of it all wrenched her heart again.

Would Kristi and Jack question the breakup? She doubted if either of them would accept the reason she'd give them. They'd pry and urge her to talk to him. Impossible. Merely seeing him again only invited more agony.

The time. All the hours she'd spent with Carlos, reveling in the sound of his voice and welcoming his touch. He'd made her feel complete, complementing her temperament with his, and she'd offered him ease and flexibility. The laughter, the Sunday mornings sharing nursery duty, the evenings they'd visited those who did not have church homes, the time they volunteered to play board games at the nursing home, and the long walks. Emptiness had crashed in with a deafening roar.

❧

Carlos wanted to call Cassidy that night, but the lateness of the hour stopped him. He considered her cell phone, but he doubted if she'd answer.

She hadn't been truthful, of that he felt certain. What had happened to shatter their dreams? If she detested him leaving for school, he'd gladly go to UT. Yet Cassidy didn't know what he'd planned, the extra money now available so he could reveal his heart. He'd made a horrible mistake. He should have told her that he loved her and mentioned the funding. They could have discussed the future together. He pounded his fist into his palm. Fury matched the ache in his heart. Nothing mattered now, unless he found out what had gone so terribly wrong.

Oh, God, have I been so blind? Was I not listening to You?

The next morning he fought the urge to call her. She needed a clear head to work and rethink the night before. He could only hope she'd change her mind and phone him.

Finding it impossible to concentrate on his job, he called

Jack at nine-thirty. Carlos needed to talk to someone about the mess he was in.

"I saw Cassidy this morning just before she left for work," Jack said. He expelled a heavy breath. "She'd been crying, and when Kristi asked what was wrong, she said you two had split up. I didn't know how soon to check on you."

"She did the splitting, and I have no clue as to why."

"Sounds like the old Cassidy reverting into her shell."

"No, Jack. She's come a long way in opening up her feelings. Something else happened, but I don't know what. Frankly, it's driving me crazy."

"Have you told her that you love her?"

"No, I was waiting," Carlos replied, suddenly feeling foolish. He wiped the perspiration from his face with his hand.

"For what?"

"I don't know, the right time and for other things to fall into place. I wanted to have a handle on grad school and funds before telling her."

"Your reasoning is as lame as Kristi and I waiting to have Walker until we could afford it. Carlos, a woman needs to know when you love her. Without a commitment, neither of you can go forward with the life God has planned for you."

"Maybe you're right," he said, staring out the window and hearing the rain pelting against the window. So reflective of his mood. "But I can't just dash into her shop and say, 'By the way I love you, so let's kiss and make up.'"

"You're a smart man. You'll come up with something," Jack said. "Best start with a prayer."

Carlos hung up the phone feeling worse than before the call. If Jack's observations were right, he'd run Cassidy off by failing to tell her how he felt. He, the one with the big sermons about communicating emotions. He, the organized, rules guy had made the worst mistake of all.

God, I need help here. Where did I go wrong? Guide me through this nightmare, please.

Shortly after lunch, he called the boutique. The moment Cassidy heard his voice, silence descended on the phone.

"Cassidy, please talk to me. Whatever the problems, we can work them out."

"I said everything last night," she replied, her voice cracking.

"Can I come by the shop at closing?"

"No. It's not a good idea, and besides I'm busy."

"How about at your house later on?"

"No. I'm packing to go out of town."

Carlos smacked his forehead. He'd forgotten her two-day market trip to Dallas. Kristi would handle things at the shop on Friday and Saturday. Cassidy planned to be back early Sunday afternoon. "What about late Sunday afternoon? We could talk then."

"It's no use. I have to go now. Customers are waiting."

She hung up without a good-bye. He hated the loneliness resonating in the silence of the phone call, the irrevocable silence. The thought of three more days without her tortured his soul. In these few short hours, he already ached with the loss.

Saturday crept by while he worked at Jack's, and he found it nearly impossible to focus on training horses. Carlos kept watching the house and the road, thinking she might come home early, and he'd be the first to catch a glimpse of her little yellow car. It didn't happen.

Kristi invited him to dinner, but he'd lost his appetite earlier in the week. Besides, he needed to check on his mother. So far he'd avoided her questions about Cassidy by stating she was out of town, but how long would it be before she discovered the truth? His mother had grown to love Cassidy. She'd be disappointed and ask questions for which he had no answers.

"You're not hungry, *mi hijo?*" she asked later that evening when he refused her offer of dinner. She frowned. "What's wrong? Missing Cassidy?"

"Something like that," he said, avoiding her gaze.

"Did you two have a quarrel?"

He sighed. "Worse than an argument. She decided we weren't right for each other."

His mother's mouth dropped open. "But. . .but she acted so happy for you the other night. Why, we talked, and I told her how good she was for you."

A suspicion inched across Carlos's mind. "What all did you talk about, Mother?"

She shook her head. "Good things about you and her. We laughed about you holding office and one day being president. I did mention I worried about how Pepe might damage your career, you know, with opponents digging up ugly things about your family."

Slowly, it all registered with him. Cassidy had acted strangely all evening, but she had not become hostile until after they'd left his mother's house. He remembered previous conversations about Cassidy's past possibly damaging his career. He thought he had taken care of her doubts then. He didn't believe the breakup had anything to do with her burden of guilt. God had removed those issues.

From what his mother now told him, Cassidy must have decided to step aside so she wouldn't hinder his career. But without Cassidy, his dreams looked meaningless. What career? His whole life lay in God's hands, and He'd already paved the way for the future.

Oh, his sweet, zany Cassidy. She did care about him, enough to call it quits rather than jeopardize his dreams. What about her hopes? He never intended for her to put aside any of her aspirations. That's why he'd wanted to make sure he had enough money as well as a job in Boston so she could pursue another boutique or continue her education—and do it as his wife.

Carlos resolved to call her every day until she agreed to see him, and one night he'd head into Austin and make a special purchase. He had money stashed away for a rainy day, and the floodgates had arrived.

By the next Sunday, Carlos had lost all patience. Every day he called Cassidy, and every day she refused to see him. That morning she'd missed Sunday school, but he saw her in church and watched her hurry out after the services. He viewed her pale skin and the dark circles beneath her eyes. Right then he resolved to visit her unannounced in the afternoon and force her to listen to what he had to say.

⁂

Cassidy ached all over. Her body refused to give in to sleep, and she had no appetite. Her boutique, which once had given her so much satisfaction, now existed only as a means of escape from Carlos's memory. But he lurked in every part of her life. Everywhere she looked, an item, a song, or the way the sun lit the sky reminded her of what she'd lost. She attempted to restore her original goals of expanding her shop so that someday she'd own a chain of affordable, fashionable dress boutiques, but the idea failed to pique her interest. God became her only source of comfort, and she clung to His promises and prayed from His Word with the hope of climbing out of her well of depression.

She couldn't attend Sunday school with her heart shattered like broken glass, neither could she act like nothing had ever existed between she and Carlos. Maybe next week or the week after, but not now. Concentrating on the worship service proved difficult enough. She felt his eyes upon her. Loving Carlos had become a part of her life, and in her resolve to renounce her selfish desires, she had to sacrifice her heart.

Cassidy swiped away a tear that she'd determined would no longer trail her every waking moment. A walk. She'd take a walk, and hopefully the warm sun would initiate healing.

Descending the stairs, she met Kristi and Uncle Jack in the kitchen. Behind them stood Carlos. The sight of him took her breath away. The crease across his forehead and the absence of his smile told her he lived in the same private agony she experienced.

"I'd like to talk," Carlos said simply.

She wanted to agree and allow herself the luxury of having his undivided presence one more time. Instead she shook her head, unable to speak.

"Would you listen to him for me?" Uncle Jack asked quietly. "I hate to see two people I love so miserable."

"Please, Honey," Kristi said in the same soft tone.

Cassidy hesitated. She glanced from Kristi to Uncle Jack and back to Carlos. How she longed to be a part of his life. "All right."

Somehow she managed to walk outside, but when his hand touched the small of her back, she felt branded, as though the world knew how much she loved him. If she'd done the right thing, why did she loathe her decision?

They strolled toward the open field where the horses grazed amid the tender grass and wildflowers. Foals, with spindly legs, jumped and played like children. Her mind held a million thoughts, none of which she could utter.

"Cassidy," he began, "I miss you."

Tears welled up in her eyes and she dared not speak. When he reached for her hand, she had no will to pull it away. His fingers entwined with hers, and he squeezed them lightly.

"I believe you miss me, too," he continued.

"It's no use," she said moistening her lips. "We won't work; our relationship is doomed before we say another word."

"Why, Cass? Tell me why."

"Because we come from two different worlds. You have plans for your life and I have mine."

"We can blend them into a perfect plan, one God would bless."

"You'd be disappointed." The call of a whippoorwill saddened her, as though the bird sympathized with her convictions.

"Never, no matter what the future holds. I would always cherish you as a gift from God."

She caught her breath and swallowed her tears. "You say

these things now, but circumstances have a way of changing our views."

"Impossible," he said with quiet deliberation. "I love you."

Her gaze flew to his face and met the truth in his dark eyes. "You love me? You can't do that, Carlos. You have to go on to school and someday run for public office. You don't have time for love. Think of the years ahead."

"I have nothing unless you're with me," he said firmly. He stopped and took her other hand in his. "I love you now and always. Nothing or no one could ever replace you."

Speechless, she had no choice but to respond to the song of her heart. "I love you, too, but I'm afraid my past will ruin your chances in politics," she said. There, she'd uttered the truth that had raged through her mind for days.

"If God ordains our dreams, nothing can stop us." He glanced around them. "I see your favorite wildflowers. I bet a few of them would bring a smile to your face."

She swallowed her tears and nibbled on her lip to keep from crumbling into a pool of tears. He strode several feet away and reached for a clump of wild yellow daisies. Suddenly he jerked his hand back and shouted.

"What is it?" she cried.

"Copperhead," he replied, grabbing his left hand. "It bit me."

Panic twisted through her body. Her eyes widened in horror. Understanding the gravity of the situation, she determined to keep a cool head. "I need to get you to the hospital," she managed to say.

He ambled her way and offered a faint smile. "It's okay, Cass. This is no big thing. I can get Jack to take me or I can drive myself."

"No," she replied, louder than she intended. "I'll take you."

To her it seemed forever before they made their way back to her car. Usually Uncle Jack or one of the trainers worked the horses this time of day, but not on a Sunday afternoon. "Wait here. I've got to get my keys. Are you okay; will you be all right here alone?"

He nodded, but he didn't convince her. Sweat beaded on his forehead, and she knew the heat hadn't caused it. Cassidy dashed inside and charged up to her room.

"What's going on?" Kristi asked from the kitchen.

"Carlos got bit by a copperhead," she said over her shoulder. "I'll call you from the hospital."

Somewhere between steering the car onto the road and uttering a perpetual prayer, she stole a glance at him. "Keep your hand down," she said, then whispered as though reminding herself, "no aspirin, no ice, no tourniquet. . ."

"Have you taken a course in first aid?" he asked lightly.

"Remember, you instructed me about snake bites after the coral snake incident. Plus, I did some reading about treatment."

He laughed and his casual approach to being bitten by a poisonous snake irritated her. "This is not funny, Carlos." She snatched up her cell phone and dialed 911. She took a deep breath and did not release it until a man answered. "I'm transporting a man to Trinity Medical Center with a snake bite. Could you alert them?"

"What kind of snake?" the man asked.

"Copperhead, and it happened about twenty minutes ago."

She replaced the phone and took another quick glimpse at him. Sweat streamed down his face.

"Smart thinking, Cass. Thanks. Is now the right time?"

"For what?"

"To ask you to marry me."

Her heart plummeted to her stomach. "You're delirious."

"Not hardly. I'm a man in love."

Her foot pressed against the accelerator, and she snatched a quick gasp of air. "You're a badly injured man, and anything you say—"

"Can and will be used against me," he finished.

A thud captured her attention. "Oh, no," she moaned, "not a flat tire." She refused to look at him. *Help me, Lord, I'm scared stiff for Carlos, and now I have to change this tire.*

"Is there any way I can help?" he asked with a weak smile.

She unfastened the seat belt and grabbed her keys from the ignition. "No, don't even consider it. Besides, it won't take me five minutes. Do you need help from the car? Does it hurt much?"

He opened the passenger side with his right hand. "I'm fine."

She knew better, but this wasn't the moment to argue with him. Unlocking the trunk, she dragged out the spare tire and her tools. How many times had she done this very thing?

"Honey, I'm sorry," he said. "I wish I could do something."

"Yeah, you can," she replied. "Don't pass out on me 'cause you're too heavy for me to lift." Her attempts at sounding humorous brought a sob. She needed to concentrate on the task at hand and pray.

Ten minutes later they were once again racing along the highway toward town. She breathed a prayer of thanks at every green light and wondered how soon before a police officer noted her speed. She whipped her car into the emergency room parking area and hurried around to open Carlos's door.

"Thanks. You did a great job in getting me here," he said, his breathing labored. "I'll be fixed in a few minutes."

"Thank me later. Let's get you inside."

She realized how quickly his strength had waned when he allowed her to help him from the car and to the emergency room entrance, where she put him in a wheelchair. His frame nearly crushed her, but she dared not complain. The profuse sweating intensified her fears. Only with God's help could she remain calm.

As soon as Carlos informed the receptionist of his snake bite, a portly nurse wheeled him directly to the examining area. Cassidy followed; the doctor would have to pick her up and throw her out before she left Carlos alone.

While Cassidy's heart pounded out a rhythm of fright, she

prayed incessantly for God's healing touch. Meanwhile the nurse washed the injury.

"I have insurance," he managed to say. "The card is in my wallet."

"We'll get to the paperwork in a few moments," the nurse replied. "Right now, let's get you comfortable."

She assisted him to a special room away from the other emergency patients and moved him to a chair beside an examining table. She took his vitals, asked pertinent questions about prior treatment for the bite, his health, the last time he ate, and allergies.

Cassidy wanted to scream. God needed to intervene. She needed desperately to see His hand in this nightmare. She watched a machine monitor Carlos's heart rate and blood pressure while the nurse measured his oxygen level.

A short, fair-haired doctor stepped in, reminding Cassidy of her dad, which helped soothe her frazzled nerves.

"I'm Dr. Rogers," he said with a smile. "I understand we have a copperhead bite here." He studied the wound. "Has the antivenin been ordered?"

"Yes, it should arrive within fifteen minutes," the nurse responded and wiped the perspiration from Carlos's face.

"We need an EKG and blood work," the doctor added.

Moments later, fluid dripped into Carlos's left arm.

"You haven't answered my question," he said.

The doctor raised a brow.

"I'm sorry; I'm talking to the young lady here." Carlos's cloudy gaze met hers. "Will you marry me?"

Dr. Rogers laughed. "How can you refuse the man?" Then he turned to Carlos. "How did you get bitten anyway?"

"Picking wildflowers," Carlos replied simply.

The doctor shook his head. "Any man who risks his life picking flowers for the woman he loves deserves a yes."

Cassidy felt tears splash over her cheeks. "Are you absolutely sure? How would we manage?"

Carlos grimaced as the doctor probed the injury. "I received enough scholarships and grants to pay for all my tuition, books, and a living allowance for married housing." He took a deep breath. "I plan on working, and with a job we could squeak by. My question is, do you want to complete your masters degree? I know your boutique means so much to you, and I don't want to take it away. That part bothers me still."

She couldn't stop the flow of emotion threatening to break into sobs. "I simply want to be with you. The boutique means nothing, and I know I could find a good job."

He frowned. "I'm not so sure I want my wife working."

"The only way I'll consider your proposal is if you let me help you."

A wide grin spread over his face. "Then the answer is yes?"

She took a deep breath. "Yes."

"Hallelujah," Dr. Rogers said with a laugh. "Hope I get an invitation since I had a part in this."

"December?" Carlos asked, closing his eyes and dampening his lips. "Can you put together your dream wedding in seven months?"

She did her best to blink back the tears now shed for happiness. "A Christmas wedding sounds wonderful."

"Doctor, could I get you to pull something out of my right pocket?"

"You're kidding," the doctor said, taking a step back. "No, I see you're not."

Carlos stretched out his leg so the doctor could draw out a tiny black velvet bag from his jeans pocket. He fished out a diamond ring and placed it in Carlos's right palm.

"Cassidy, this is not how I'd planned to ask you to marry me, but I promise to do it all properly on our wedding day."

"I don't care; it's perfect." And they laughed at her emphasis on *perfect*.

She watched as he slipped the symbol of their love on her

finger and held her hand firmly in his. "I love you, Cassidy, and I want to spend the rest of my life with you."

Elation rose through her from the bottom of her toes. "And I love you, Carlos Diaz, and I will marry you. Something tells me our life together will be anything but dull."

"I promise you will always be the first lady of my heart," he said.

The door opened and a nurse handed the doctor a vial.

"Go ahead and kiss her before the nurse starts the anti-venin," the doctor said. "I want this proposal to be one I never forget."

Carlos stared up with the incredible smile that had won her over the first day he'd walked into her boutique. She leaned over and saw a reflection of herself in his dark eyes seconds before he brushed a kiss across her lips.

twenty-two

Six months later, December 18

"I have never been so nervous in my whole life," Carlos said. "Is this tie straight?"

Jack straightened the shirt of the tux and centered the bow tie. "I well remember—my heart hammered in my ears like a timpani."

"More like cannon fire," Carlos said. "You have the ring, right? I mean I did give it to you, right?"

Jack patted his jacket pocket. "It's here, just like the last three times you asked me. Do you need any words of wisdom?"

Carlos peered into his friend's face. "I don't think so. Y'all have given me enough advice for a lifetime."

"That's because a marriage is for a lifetime."

Carlos nodded and felt a nervous smile tug at his lips. "Thanks for everything—being best man and taking care of Cassidy while I was at school this first semester."

"No problem. You know, I've become rather attached to my niece, and now you're taking her off to Boston."

"We'll be back for visits." He felt a shiver race up his spine. "Do you suppose she's as nervous as I am?"

"Knowing Cassidy, she's pacing the floor."

❧

"Sweetheart, can't you stop pacing?" her mother asked with an exasperated sigh.

Cassidy took a deep breath and stopped in the middle of the hardwood floor. "No. Can't. It's impossible. My stomach is hatching butterflies, a million a minute." She glanced about the Victorian-styled bedroom of the Country Charm Bed and Breakfast. "Do you suppose the guests downstairs can hear me?"

Kristi laughed and reached out to brush back one of Cassidy's loose curls. "I'm sure they can hear all ninety-five pounds of you."

Cassidy stared at her trembling fingers. "I do appreciate your mom and dad hosting my wedding here. I remember when you and Jack got married. Everything went beautifully."

"Mom knows you're grateful," Kristi replied, "and she loves planning events."

"The entire house is lovely with the Christmas decorations," Cassidy's mother added. "At first I couldn't believe my daughter chose this time of year to marry, but with all the love and excitement in the air, the timing is perfect."

Perfect, Cassidy thought. "I wonder how Carlos is doing? He seldom gets nervous."

"Do you want me to go check?" Carly asked, smoothing her deep green gown over her slender body.

"No," her mother quickly interjected. "You stay right here where I can keep an eye on you."

Carly winked at Cassidy. "She's afraid I'll run off with the groom."

"Sorry, I don't share, Sis," Cassidy said. She shrugged happily. "God is so good. He brought me here to such wonderful family and friends, Carlos, and now a wedding."

Her mother shook her head and offered a faint smile. "With all of these blessings, I still can't believe Thelma purchased your boutique," her mother said. "But God does have a way of working things out."

"He sure does, and Thelma's daughter Rachel has really made a turnaround."

A knock on the door interrupted them. When her father stepped inside, Cassidy could hear the soft sounds of the piano playing a Latino love song.

"It's time," he said, holding out his hands to take hers. "Are you ready?"

"Yep, we're prayed up, prettied up, and ready to go," Cassidy said with a nervous laugh.

Her mother graced her cheek with a kiss and blinked back tears. "You look absolutely stunning," she whispered. "My baby all grown up. . . . I'll be downstairs waiting. I love you."

Cassidy mouthed the same endearing words, afraid an utterance would bring an onslaught of emotion. Carly and Kristi touched a kiss upon her cheek before heading into the hallway.

"Is my girl ready to become Mrs. Carlos Diaz?" her father asked.

"I think so, Dad. I just wish I didn't feel so nervous."

"Carlos is a mess."

"My Carlos?" she asked bewildered.

"The same." He hesitated as the piano began the processional.

"Honey, we can't cry, but I want to say how proud I am of you and how very much I love you."

Cassidy took a deep breath to regain her composure. "Thank you, and I do love you so very much."

They positioned themselves in the hall, and when the piano began the traditional wedding march, signaling the arrival of the bride, they began their descent. She tingled from her head to her feet, and for a moment she feared she might be sick. Her dad placed his hand over hers in the crook of his arm. Silently she conveyed how much she depended on his strength.

Thank You, Lord. Bless this day and all who share in our celebration of marriage.

Midway down the winding staircase, her eyes met Carlos's. Oh, how she loved this man and everything about him. He found so much joy in serving the Lord, and she never ceased to revel in his love for her. From across the room she could see his dark eyes were moist, and the moment nearly reduced her to a puddle of tears.

Suddenly she hooked her toe on the front of her white satin gown. Cassidy gasped, feeling herself ready to topple down the stairs in front of all the smiling guests. In one smooth motion, her dad righted her steps.

With a deep breath she continued on. Her life with Carlos would hold more than a trip or two, but as long as the heavenly Father straightened their steps, they'd have a beautiful life together.

A Letter To Our Readers

Dear Reader:

In order that we might better contribute to your reading enjoyment, we would appreciate your taking a few minutes to respond to the following questions. We welcome your comments and read each form and letter we receive. When completed, please return to the following:

Rebecca Germany, Fiction Editor
Heartsong Presents
PO Box 719
Uhrichsville, Ohio 44683

1. Did you enjoy reading *Cassidy's Charm* by DiAnn Mills?
   ☐ Very much! I would like to see more books
   by this author!
   ☐ Moderately. I would have enjoyed it more if

   _____

   _____

   _____

2. Are you a member of **Heartsong Presents**? Yes ☐ No ☐
   If no, where did you purchase this book?_____

   _____

3. How would you rate, on a scale from 1 (poor) to 5 (superior), the cover design?_____

4. On a scale from 1 (poor) to 10 (superior), please rate the following elements.

   _____ Heroine   _____ Plot

   _____ Hero   _____ Inspirational theme

   _____ Setting   _____ Secondary characters

5. These characters were special because _____

_____

_____

6. How has this book inspired your life? _____

_____

_____

7. What settings would you like to see covered in future
   Heartsong Presents books? _____

_____

_____

8. What are some inspirational themes you would like to see
   treated in future books? _____

_____

_____

9. Would you be interested in reading other **Heartsong
   Presents** titles?   Yes ❑   No ❑

10. Please check your age range:
    ❑ Under 18   ❑ 18-24   ❑ 25-34
    ❑ 35-45   ❑ 46-55   ❑ Over 55

Name _____

Occupation _____

Address _____

City _____ State _____ Zip _____

Email _____

NEW ENGLAND

From the majestic mountains to the glorious seashore, experience the beauty New England offers the romantic heart. Four respected authors will take you on an unforgettable trip with true-to-life characters.

Here's your ticket for a refreshing escape to the Northeast. Enjoy the view as God works His will in the lives of those who put their trust in Him.

paperback, 476 pages, 5 ³⁄₁₆" x 8"

❤ ❤ ❤ ❤ ❤ ❤ ❤ ❤ ❤ ❤ ❤ ❤ ❤ ❤ ❤ ❤ ❤ ❤ ❤

❤ ❤ ❤ ❤ ❤ ❤ ❤ ❤ ❤ ❤ ❤ ❤ ❤ ❤ ❤ ❤ ❤ ❤ ❤

one

Darting into the middle of West Alamo Street while vehicles honked and rolled to a screeching halt was not the wisest course of action in Brenham, Texas. But for Cassidy Frazier, practically oblivious to the sights and sounds around her, this moment marked the epitome of her newly established career. Shielding her eyes to peer up at the newly painted sign above her boutique, she broke into a wide grin.

"I love it," she called up to her uncle Jack, who sat perched on a ladder with a can of paint. She scrutinized every letter, the swirl and design tickling her creative instincts.

"Cassidy, get out of the street, or you'll spend the opening day of your shop at the friendly funeral home," he shouted, twisting his back as though it ached.

As if to reinforce Uncle Jack's warning, an angry driver began heckling her. Cassidy mouthed an apology and hurried to the sidewalk. "The sign is perfect," she said, waving at her uncle's scowling face. "Come down and see for yourself."

He climbed down the ladder, maintaining a precarious grip on a can of royal blue paint and holding a brush by its handle in his teeth.

"Stand back here with me," she said. "It's breathtaking."

"Not in the street," Uncle Jack said, sounding very much like her father instead of her youthful uncle. He took a few steps backward to the edge of the sidewalk.

"Cassidy's Charm," she read, pride swelling in her voice. "Just look at the way the C loops and curls." She cupped her left hand and traced an imaginary C. "This looks better than script. It's rather old-worldish, don't you think?"

"As long as you're happy," Uncle Jack said, swiping at the

droplets of perspiration on his brow in the early August heat. Wet, straw-colored hair plastered against his reddened face, and with his short stature he more closely resembled a teen than a grown man.

"I'll get you a towel and a bottle of water," she said and dashed inside her shop. The smell of fresh wood and new clothes greeted her. Racks of artfully displayed, fashionable apparel lined the walls and circled the middle of the store. Mannequins clothed in casual attire, dresses, and sport ensembles were accessorized with scarves and stunning jewelry, then positioned in decorated corners and other strategic spots throughout the room. The boutique did have a unique country-chic charm, and she couldn't wait for tomorrow's first day of business.

"Cassidy, did you get lost?" Uncle Jack asked, weariness edging his voice. "I'm dying in this heat, and I don't think you want me smelling up your place or tracking in paint."

Cringing, she hurried to the back of the shop. She grabbed a water bottle from the compact refrigerator and pulled a towel from a storage drawer. "I'm coming," she replied, racing to the entrance.

Uncle Jack stood in the doorway and eagerly accepted the towel, then twisted off the cap to the bottle. "I know why you took so long," he said with a wry grin.

"Why is that?"

"You were admiring your store."

"Boutique," she corrected and feigned annoyance. "And you're right." Excitement again rippled through her body. "My boutique will be the rage of Brenham. Every lady, young and old, will clamor to get inside." She rubbed her palms together in anticipation.

"According to my wife, you're right," Uncle Jack said after gulping down some of the cold water.

"But I couldn't have accomplished a thing without you and Kristi pushing me in the right direction," Cassidy replied, "and

providing me a place to stay until I can get an apartment." She threw her arms around his neck. "Thank you, Uncle Jack. I'll be a success, and you will be so proud of me."

"I'm already proud without all of this froufrou stuff." He took another swig of water. "You're going to have to do something about your accent. The New Yawk Yankee talk won't cut it in Texas."

She released her hold on his neck and laughed. "You are one to critique *my* accent," she protested. "Yours is just as bad. Besides, I've been practicing my drawl."

"Won't work. I've been here four years and I'm still labeled as talking funny."

"I'll practice harder." She planted a kiss on his cheek and urged him to remove his shoes and step inside to cooler temperatures. "Now that everything is in order, you can go back to running your horse farm and being husband and daddy without worrying about all my pre-opening jitters."

The bell jingled above the door, and Kristi stepped in, carrying her and Jack's young son. "Hi," she greeted. "The sign looks great. I'd wondered about your choice of blue, but it looks more navy—and great against the tan background."

Uncle Jack scooped a wide-awake, nine-month-old Walker from his mother's arms. "How's my boy?" he asked.

"Wet," Kristi replied, pulling a scrunchie from her purse to tie back her shoulder-length dark hair. "Can I change him in the back room, Cass?"

"Go right ahead," Cassidy replied, making faces at the baby and coaxing a giggle from him. She took a second look at Kristi's small shoulder bag. "Where did you get that purse? It's adorable."

Kristi smiled and patted it. "Carlos Diaz gave it to me for my birthday."

Cassidy reached out to touch the intricate leather. "I've never seen anything like this before. Look at the delicate, feminine design. Wonder where he got it? Is the name brand inside?"

"No, it's unique, and you won't be able to find it at market. Carlos makes them," Kristi said, pulling out a diaper from the folds of the baby carrier.

"You're kidding," Cassidy replied, her curiosity piqued. "Does he have a shop?"

"No." Kristi turned to her husband. "Why don't you explain Carlos while I change our son?"

Uncle Jack handed her the baby, wrinkling his nose. "Sounds more pleasant than dealing with whatever's causing that odor." He watched mother and son disappear into the back room. Pride etched his face and tugged at the corners of his mouth.

"Okay, Cass," he said, turning back to her. "Carlos makes these purses, wallets for men and women, and belts for all ages. It's a hobby."

"So he does this when he's not working for you?" Cassidy asked.

"Among other things. He just completed college at A&M in three years, and he's a recipient of the Truman Scholarship."

"I thought he trained horses for you."

"He does, when he's not busy with a ton of other things. He'll be heading off to grad school a year from now."

Cassidy glanced around at an empty display case where she'd planned to carry accessories. "I haven't found a line of leather goods to meet my price range and quality requirements. Do you suppose he'd be interested in supplying me with those things? Although he does sound busy." She lifted a brow. "Haven't I met him?"

"Possibly. He attended our wedding, and he's in and out at the ranch. But I'll see him this afternoon and ask him to give you a call."

"Great. He can stop by the store anytime. I'll be here from morning to night." She whirled around to drink in another view of her dream come true. "Hmm. A local craftsman would be great for my business and his."

She tried to remember meeting Carlos, but her mind drew a blank. Oh, well, she'd know soon enough.

ॐ

Carlos Diaz signed his name and wrote in "August 2" at the bottom of the University of Texas's grad school scholarship application, then slipped it into a manila envelope along with the other required information. He'd completed the forms well ahead of the deadline because he detested having things hang over his head. Ever since he'd heard and read the glowing reports about UT's law and public policy program, he'd been interested. He felt confident about his chances to receive additional financial aid to help with the Truman Scholarship, especially with his four point grade average and ethnic background, but that didn't stop the apprehension he felt every time he thought about leaving his ailing mother.

Of course, if Isabella Diaz ever got wind of the idea that her son hesitated to complete his masters because of her diabetes, she'd chase him with a switch. His mother, a fiercely independent and feisty Mexican-born woman, insisted her six children obtain their college degrees and more. To her, education was a God-given responsibility.

If UT accepted him, he'd have to live in Austin. He couldn't run home every day to check on her, and she simply refused to follow the diet needed to keep her in good health. Just last week, he'd offered to cook dinner only to find a bag of peanut bars stuffed in the back of her pantry.

His mother had said she kept them for children at the church, but Carlos didn't believe her for one minute. How could he consider moving away from the area when he couldn't trust her to follow doctor's simple orders? Her habits frustrated and worried him. She denied her medical condition and worked at her clerk's job far too many hours. What would it take for her to pay attention to her health?

Carlos shock his head and stole a glance at his watch— three o'clock. Two days ago, Jack had told him about his

niece's new boutique and her interest in his leather goods. He'd promised to stop in and show her some of his pieces. At first, he'd toyed with constructing the leather items as a way of preserving his father's and grandfather's memory as craftsmen, but it might be profitable after all. Even with the generous wages earned from working at Jack's horse ranch, he still had to budget his money.

Snatching up his keys, Carlos grabbed a box of neatly stacked leather goods. The trek to the shop should only take a few minutes. He remembered Cassidy Frazier from over three-and-a-half years ago at Jack and Kristi's Valentine's Day wedding. At the time, he'd thought the petite blond looked a bit too pale and thin, but she did have a quick laugh and easy smile.

He grinned, recalling her near fall as she tripped while going down the steps of the bed and breakfast owned by Kristi's parents. Standing near the bannister, he'd caught her arm, saving her from toppling head first into a row of guests.

"Thanks," she'd whispered, her face mirroring the elegant red gown. "Nothing like a grand entrance."

Carlos chuckled at his musings. Seeing Cassidy again would be entertaining, if she remembered him at all. Although she now lived with Jack and Kristi, their paths hadn't crossed since her move to Brenham in June.

Taking another quick look at his watch, he locked his apartment door and headed toward his truck, glimmering in the afternoon sun. One thing he firmly believed: A clean truck indicated a clean life.

Moments later, he swung into a parking space on West Alamo Street. Couldn't miss her shop with the huge Cassidy's Charm sign. He remembered Jack saying something about painting it for her in an outlandish shade of blue. Traveling across the country and opening a shop at Cassidy's age took a lot of spunk for one little lady. From what Jack said, she couldn't be much more than twenty-two years old.

Carrying the box of leather goods, Carlos watched the grand opening banner flutter in the late summer breeze. Another sign invited shoppers to select purchases with a twenty-five percent discount and boasted free refreshments. Now that would attract women.

She'd chosen a great location across from the Washington County Courthouse. The shop, or rather boutique as Kristi called it, hummed with activity, a giggle here, a laugh there, a hearty "You look absolutely stunning," and an "I need my control-top panty hose."

It took only a few seconds to confirm his fears: He was the only man within sight or earshot. Carlos gulped. Maybe none of the women would notice him.

The smell of vanilla cappuccino filled the air, and when he turned his gaze toward the source of that sweet coffee scent, he saw a huge tray of cookies and muffins. They looked homemade. *Ah*, he thought, his taste buds watering as he read a fancy scripted sign propped against a vase of daisies: Compliments of the Country Charm Bed and Breakfast. His aunt Irene, who worked for the B&B, baked the best cookies and muffins in Texas, although he didn't dare voice that opinion in his mother's presence.

In a far corner, he heard Cassidy. He couldn't see her, only hear her delightful New York accent. Craning his neck, he spied the top of her curly blond head.

Carlos didn't know whether to wait or leave. His schedule for the rest of the week was packed tighter than a jar of pickles, and spending time in a shop full of women made him feel less than comfortable. Hopefully none of them would emerge from a dressing room half-clad to search for additional clothing to try on.

He spotted a chair beside the refreshment table. Hmm, he could set his box on the floor and enjoy one of Aunt Irene's cookies. Too bad he hadn't brought a book to read. Mother had just presented him with a biography of Winston Churchill,

and he itched to get into it.

With a sigh, he realized the boutique stayed open until five o'clock. He had an hour to wait unless these droves of women bought out the store and headed home.

"How do you think this looks?" a matronly woman asked.

Carlos tilted his head and decided to reserve his opinion of the bright pink-and-orange ankle-length tunic with fringe hanging nearly to the floor. He liked the black pants and knit top underneath it better.

"I mean with the right shoes and jewelry, of course," the woman continued. "My husband is coming home from a business trip tomorrow, and I wanted to surprise him with something different."

Dear Lord. What have You gotten me into? Help me before I make a terrible mistake.

"I'm sure he'll be so glad to see you that it won't matter what you wear," Carlos replied, feeling the hair on his neck stand on end.

"Oh, you are so sweet," she cooed and wagged her finger. "I'll take this for sure." She padded away, and he breathed a sigh of relief before he heard her say, "Ladies, there is a good-looking young man over by the refreshment table. He looks just like that Latino singer, the one with the fantastic smile, and he gave me the best advice. . . . Oh, you don't know if this looks nice on you? Go ask that young man I just spoke about. He has excellent taste."

During the next hour, twenty, thirty, maybe a hundred women paced before Carlos, seeking his guidance on their treasured finds. He tried to be tactful and complimentary, but some choices were awful. Not once did he see Cassidy.

Finally only one woman remained in the store. He stood, and Cassidy waved from the dressing area. "I'll be right with you," she said with a smile. "You're Carlos, aren't you?"

"Yes, that's me."

"You're great for business," she called in a melodious lilt.

"My customers loved your comments."

"Glad they did," he muttered.

"What?"

"Never mind. I'll set my things on the counter."

Carlos studied a tabletop display of silver jewelry. The pieces were of superior quality, but someone had arranged them haphazardly, some on little black velvet boxes and others placed beside them or left dangling. At last he could be of some help. It only took a few minutes to pull them off the velvet boxes and then line all the pieces in nice, straight rows. Pleased with his efforts, he glanced about to see if he could be of further use. The ladies trying on clothes must have messed up everything for poor Cassidy.

An antique-white kitchen cabinet framed with an ivy vine grabbed his attention. Cassidy had a varied assortment of bath products positioned there. In no time at all, Carlos had rearranged the items according to height and type of product.

Next, three shelves of lightweight knit tops captured his attention. At least Cassidy's customers hadn't destroyed this. Poor girl, if he hadn't been available, she'd have been stuck straightening her whole store.

At the refreshment table, he wrapped a napkin around his fingers and carefully stacked each cookie and muffin on the tray side by side.

"What has happened?" Cassidy asked, seizing his attention. The look on her face spoke of sheer surprise. "Who rearranged all my displays?"

Carlos smiled. "You're welcome. I fixed them for you since I'm sure you had a long day."

Cassidy's gaze flitted from one of his projects to another. The woman behind her broke into hysterical laughter.

"You did this?" Cassidy asked, her blue gray eyes widening and her tiny body quivering beneath the skirt of her sun-yellow suit. Her hand gestured around the shop. "Why?"

two

Cassidy shivered. She wanted to explode, unleash her temper and dive in for the kill, but the man before her had the most adorable, innocent look about him.

"Why?" he repeated. "To help you out, so you wouldn't get stuck working until after dark putting your shop back together."

"Oh," she said and prayed God would take pliers to her tongue. "I really prefer having the items the other way."

"You do?" He sighed. "Looks like I just made a wonderful impression. Okay, I'll put them back."

"No." The words tumbled out of her mouth a little louder than she intended. "I mean, no thanks. I'll do it before I go home or in the morning."

The lady behind Cassidy continued to laugh. "Oh, my," she said as tears rolled down her ample cheeks. "Best let me pay for these things before you two go at it."

Cassidy slowly turned and presented as pleasant a demeanor as possible to her customer. "I'd be happy to ring up your purchases."

The woman handed Cassidy a credit card and rummaged through Carlos's box. "What smart looking purses, and my daughter could use a couple of these belts. Are you planning to carry these?"

At that particular moment, the idea of using Carlos as a vendor held as much appeal as listening to her uncle Jack talk about snakes in the horse barn. "Possibly," she said, standing perfectly poised for the credit card machine to post its approval.

Once the woman left the store, Cassidy locked the front

door and affixed the closed sign in the storefront window. All the while she bit back the sarcasm threatening to unleash itself on Mr. Carlos Diaz and his viewpoints about the display of fashions and accessories. Her courses at college hadn't covered this.

Glancing back at the dark-haired man standing awkwardly among the feminine clothing and all the things that went with it, she suddenly found the whole incident hilarious.

"I'm glad you find this funny," he said, easing his box to the floor. "I feel like a fool."

She crossed the room, hearing her laughter whip around the boutique. "It's all of it—the women clinging to you for advice and the way you attempted to help me straighten up. Priceless."

"Shall we start over?" he asked, jamming his hands into his jeans. "I can walk out and come back in carrying my box of wares with nothing to distract me."

"And miss the way you handled my customers? Not on your life." She reached out to shake his hand, but neglected to navigate the box sitting on the floor between them. She tripped and lunged forward, falling straight into Carlos's open arms. Once he helped her to her feet, she stared into his eyes—huge, nearly black pools of warmth and merriment. She'd seen those eyes before.

"Now I know where we met," she said, tugging at her jacket.

Carlos grinned, revealing a dimple on his right cheek. "Jack and Kristi's wedding. You were coming down the stairs— "

"I remember," she replied, feeling less than confident about their first encounter. "I nearly made a scene in front of a room full of guests." She recalled how the red gown had dipped dangerously low when she fell forward. Wow, what a first impression she'd made. Now she and Carlos were even.

Taking a deep breath, as daintily as possible, she began. "I love your craftsmanship." *Why did I say love? He'll think*

I'm a ditsy blond for sure. "I don't believe I've seen such quality work." She selected a soft brown belt trimmed in silver studs. "I'd like to carry them in my boutique, if we can agree on a price."

He nodded and smiled. "I'm not out to make a killing on these."

Why didn't she remember those incredible white teeth? "Good, which is why I haven't purchased a line of purses, belts, or wallets yet. I want good quality but at an affordable price. I like the idea of having a local person supply me with merchandise, plus the exposure is good for both of us."

Shortly thereafter they came to terms on the cost and delivery date. Cassidy relaxed slightly as Carlos explained the history of the craftsmanship handed down from his grandfather and father. He wanted to preserve their memory and carry on their legacy.

"Uncle Jack tells me you just graduated from college."

"Sure did, last May. Wish I had settled in my mind to get my schooling a little sooner, but I worked two years prior to beginning my freshman year."

"For Uncle Jack, right?"

"Yes. Another love of mine is horses, especially the Arabians on your uncle Jack's ranch. Problem is, I enjoy lots of things—you know, Jack-of-all trades, master of none." He leaned against the counter on one elbow. He looked about five foot ten or so, certainly a tower of height over her. When she stood as straight as possible, she barely reached the five-foot mark.

Cassidy felt her stomach do a little flip from his nearness. "Looks to me like you're a master of quite a bit. I hear you are a Truman Scholar. Where do you plan to attend grad school?"

He appeared to contemplate his answer. Not really sure. "God's been tugging at me about that, and I believe I'm heading in the right direction."

"And what does He want you to do?"

"Politics," Carlos replied without hesitation. "I'd like a degree in law and public policy."

Stunned, Cassidy didn't know how to reply. This guy was definitely not what she expected.

"You're surprised," he said with a chuckle, his dimple deepening. "You're not the first." He bent to the floor and carefully lined up his leather goods in their box, which he then hoisted into his arms. "Thanks for the interest in my things. I'll put it all together and swing by tomorrow morning on my way out of town."

"Good. I can start to sell them right away." She walked him toward the front of the shop.

"I've succeeded in talking about myself and not finding out a thing about you," he said. "Next time you'll have to tell me all about yourself. By the way, are you attending church with Jack and Kristi?" He paused at the door, and when she nodded, he continued. "I think you'd like the young adult Sunday school class—an excellent opportunity to meet new people, too."

"Thanks, I think I will. Truthfully, I've done little else but work since I arrived two months ago."

He gave her another death-defying smile. "I'd be happy to introduce you to the others."

Cassidy wanted to watch Carlos maneuver the box to his vehicle but decided a professional relationship didn't leave room for personal considerations. At least her reasoning sounded good.

What a strange man with his eccentric obsession about arranging things. He was definitely diverse in his interests, but everything she saw reeked of perfectionism. A man like that would drive her crazy, and she hoped they could work together without a problem. Did he say law and public policy? And he thought God wanted him in politics? Yuck! How boring. It bordered on working in environmental development

or statistics. She shrugged and picked up a misplaced silver necklace. Well, somebody had to run the country. Luckily for her and the rest of the world, God hadn't chosen her.

ॐ

Carlos laughed all the way back to his apartment. What a zany girl. Those huge blue gray eyes and her petite frame would snag the attention of every available male in Brenham. In short, she was drop-dead gorgeous and apparently had a mind for business, but she'd drive him crazy with her clumsiness and her compulsion to arrange things with as much of a sense of order as kids putting away their toys. The New York accent sounded cuter coming from her than from Jack. It gave her individuality. He wondered how he'd missed her at Jack's ranch and at church.

He drove out of town onto a country road en route to his mother's home. She thought he needed another home-cooked meal, but he really wanted to monitor her eating and make sure she'd taken her insulin. His five brothers and sisters had offered repeatedly to take over the responsibility of their mother, but they had families of their own. Besides, if he didn't take care of the matter himself, he'd worry it hadn't been handled correctly.

His spry mother met him at the door, wearing an apron and drying her hands. *"Mi hijo*, my son, you look handsome as ever."

He grinned and gave her a hug. "Hmm, I smell something wonderful, and I'm starved."

She stepped back and took a proud look at him. "Good, there are plenty of enchiladas and your favorite cream cake for dessert."

Carlos frowned. "Mama, I told you nothing sweet. I'm watching my weight, and you can't have the sugar."

"Nonsense." She placed her hands on her slender hips. "You're far from fat, and I intend to send the cake home with you anyway."

He removed his baseball cap and wrapped an arm around

her narrow shoulders. They ambled into the kitchen, where the rich, spicy smells of dinner sent his taste buds soaring. They talked all during dinner. He told her about the boutique carrying his leather goods but not about his rearrangement of Cassidy's things. As usual, they spoke as though they hadn't seen each other in weeks when it had been only a day since they'd last spoken.

"Tell me," she said, pouring both of them a coffee refill. "Have you read the book about Winston Churchill yet?"

"Just started it," he replied, staring at the huge slice of cream cake. "I wanted to reread C. S. Lewis's *Mere Christianity* before diving into a new one."

"I see," she replied with a smile. "A difficult book for me to understand, but not too difficult for my educated son."

Carlos laughed and lifted his fork to his mouth. He already anticipated the vanilla flavor and generous mound of frosting sending his taste buds straight to heaven. "Great cake, Mom. And I'm taking it home, right?"

"Of course, unless you want to leave it here for when you stop by."

"No, I'll take it with me," he replied, understanding if the dessert stayed, his mother would eat a piece or two.

"Have you decided on where you plan to attend grad school? After all, I don't want you to lose your Truman Scholarship," she said, eyeing him over the top of her coffee cup. "I heard you wanted to go to Harvard."

He raised a brow. "Mother, I won't lose my status as a Truman Scholar. I just need to select a grad school. How did you know about Harvard, anyway?"

"From your aunt Irene. She heard it from Kristi's mother, who must have heard it from Kristi, which means Jack knew and you must have told him. Why must I be the last one to know these things? A mother should be the first."

Carlos reached for her callused hand. "I wanted to surprise you, and if I didn't get the funding, then you wouldn't be

disappointed. I'm sorry if I hurt your feelings."

"Somehow I think there's more to this than what you're telling me." Her dark eyes clouded. "Where is this school?"

"Well, I think the two offering the best programs for law and public policy are Harvard and the University of Texas," he said slowly. "Naturally, UT in Austin would be my best choice."

"Why there? Aren't you limiting yourself?"

Carlos stifled an exasperated sigh. "I prefer to stay close to home."

"A very bad excuse, *mi hijo*. How long will it take for you to get this degree?"

"Four years," he said, the cake rapidly losing its appeal.

"I'll pray," she announced firmly. "God always hears a mother's prayer first."

Carlos chuckled. "I don't think you'll find that doctrine in the Bible. What else have you been praying for?"

"Oh, small things. . .like a nice girl for my Carlos, one who will temper his strange, set ways."

"Mother, you said I acted just like Dad, and you liked it."

She set her cup on its saucer. "I loved your father, Carlos, but not every trait about him. Much to my regret, you are worse." She crossed her arms on the table and continued seriously. "Look at how you eat cake. Each bite is exactly the same size as the one before."

Bewildered, he immediately began to analyze his mother's statement. It wasn't the first time she or someone else had pointed out his behavior. His sisters called him quirky, his brothers called him weird, and his aunt Irene referred to him as peculiar, but Carlos thought his actions amounted to plain logic. Everything had a place, and every place had a purpose.

"Mother, I don't see a thing wrong with my habits."

She lifted her chin as though facing an audience. "Perhaps you should pray and see if your insistence upon things being done in a particular way is what God has in mind for you."

She leaned closer into the table. "Sometimes we need to see the beauty in creativity, just like we need to see the good in the worst of people. You act as though your way is the only way things ought to be done."

"It's the best way."

"Excellence knows no master."

He instantly raised a brow. "Mother, you're quoting Plato."

"Yes, *The Republic,* book ten. I can read, you know." She sat straighter and stirred her coffee. "Mark my word, *mi hijo,* you will have an ulcer by the time you're thirty and heart problems by the time you're thirty-five if you don't find the beauty in life."

Carlos felt frustration seep through his skin. In his estimation, an undisciplined life had a lot to do with his mother's diabetes and his father's untimely death due to alcoholism. He intended to lead a healthy, ordered life, with God's help of course.

"And furthermore, I would appreciate it if you would stop by to see your mother because you love her, not because you're checking to see if she's following her diet and taking her medication."

three

Carlos nearly choked on his cake. "I do love you, Mother, which is why I want to make sure you're taking good care of yourself. Guess I could have been a little more discreet, but you don't do what the doctor mandates."

She shook her head and pursed her lips. "No child of mine is going to be saddled with looking after me. I refuse to be a burden."

"You are not—"

"I'm not finished yet," she said, instantly silencing him as she narrowed her gaze. "Now, why haven't you applied to Harvard? Wouldn't a degree from there establish your credibility as a politician?"

"I hadn't looked into it," he said sheepishly.

"Then do it," she said and accented her words with a sweet smile. "Now, let's finish our meal. So when are you taking the leather goods to the boutique?"

Carlos left his mother's home shortly after eight-thirty. The comment she made about his habits bothered him. In the past, she'd defended him when others made fun of or criticized his mannerisms. Tonight she'd surprised him, and he wondered if his habits had grown worse as he worked toward his goal of ordered, disciplined living. *Maybe I'm getting old. After all, I'm twenty-four; next year my car insurance premium goes down.* He shifted in his truck seat, and wiped away a piece of invisible dust on the dashboard, then flipped on the overhead light to ensure his hair looked good.

His orderly environment suited him fine. Someday he'd be asking people to vote him into public office. They'd need to rely on a man whose feet were firmly rooted in Christ and

would go to great lengths to help people. He had so many things he wanted to do, especially in the way of assisting minorities to reach their full potential. Surely his ways would not hinder him from accomplishing his dreams. He wanted people to see a Latino man who cared about others and desired to do whatever it took for the job. But voters—and his family—needed to see a likeable sort of guy, not one labeled fastidious or strange.

"Okay, Lord," Carlos said aloud. "If I need to tone down my ways, let me know."

At that instant, he slammed on his brakes and swerved his pickup to keep from hitting a deer. He hit the steering wheel with the heel of his hand. "All right, Lord," he said, shaking his head. "You have my attention."

❧

Cassidy put the finishing touches on straightening her shop at precisely 9:58 A.M., two minutes before the boutique opened. She yawned and stretched, regretting the mere eight hours of sleep she'd managed the previous night. Normally nine or more suited her better. She seized her keys and sighed happily. God was so good to bless her with this chance to prove to her mom and dad she indeed could be responsible and run a business.

No sooner had she adjusted the banner announcing her opening week than Carlos arrived with his leather goods. She hadn't yet decided if their differences might conflict with a good professional relationship. But, she reasoned, their contact should be minimal. No problem, as long as he didn't insist upon his own display method.

Cassidy muffled a giggle. Kristi and Uncle Jack had laughed all evening about yesterday's incident, and after a while, so had she. It's all about the people business, she told herself. Some are real challenges. Carlos may be talented and good looking, but he could try a saint's patience.

"Good morning, Cassidy." Carlos's voice brought her back

to the present. "I've brought everything we discussed."

"Thank you," she said and yawned. "Please excuse me. I'm not awake yet."

He smiled.

Where did he get those dazzling white teeth?

"I've been up for hours," he said, pulling a list of the merchandise, in duplicate, from his shirt pocket.

"Figures," she replied, quickly adding her own smile to buffer her wayward tongue. She glanced through the assortment. "These are beautiful. I'm really excited about this."

"While you sort through them, I need to get something else from my truck."

She picked up a small shoulder purse, its silver work closely resembling embroidery. Laying it aside, she decided it must be hers. One by one she lifted the purses, wallets, and belts from the box, each one impressing her with its uniqueness. No two were alike, but all were beautifully crafted. Cassidy recalled Carlos telling her the work had been handed down from his grandfather in Mexico. What a rich family heritage.

The bell jingled over the front door, and she lifted her gaze to see Carlos carrying a bouquet of miniature red roses and a small, ribbon-covered box.

"For you," he said, handing her the lovely flowers and placing the box on the counter.

Thoroughly delighted, she noted the fresh scent waltzing around the shop. "How sweet of you. Thank you so much."

"Well, after yesterday, I thought I needed to redeem myself," he said and nodded toward the box. "Hopefully this will help, too."

Cassidy loved gifts; they always revealed a lot about a person's character. She glanced into his face and untied the gold ribbon from around the box. "My favorite," she said with a laugh, gazing down at the milk chocolates resting in white delicate paper cups. "How did you know I cannot resist

chocolate?" she asked, carefully examining each piece to see which one she'd eat first.

"Oh, an uncle of yours," he replied. "He said chocolate would cure anything that ails you."

She flashed him a knowing look. "He's right—it's almost as good as a prayer. Thank you so much, but it really wasn't necessary."

"Oh, yes, it was. You put all your time and effort into your shop, and I came along and undid your work."

"Don't forget all those ladies bought clothes because you took the time to give them special attention," she said, selecting a chocolate and offering him one.

He shook his head to decline the candy. "I won't do that again, either. Talk about diplomatic procedures." He scanned the lists, which she'd already signed and pulled a pen from his shirt pocket.

"Hmm, you're left-handed," she noted.

"It depends on the mood I'm in," he said as he scribbled his signature.

"Uncle Jack claims you're super intelligent," she said, recalling somewhere in the recesses of her mind something about ambidextrous people having superior minds."

"Don't know about the truth of his observations," Carlos said, sticking his pen back into his pocket and folding his copy of their transaction. "But I have him fooled." He graced her with another superb smile. "I'll see you at Sunday school?" he asked.

"Oh, yes. I'll be there."

After he left, she helped herself to a cup of cappuccino. Between the roses, the candy, and the coffee, the shop smelled heavenly. She stretched with one hand and selected another chocolate. Carlos might drive her nuts, but he did know how to bring nice gifts.

The day passed quickly, ending her first week in business. Cassidy was overjoyed with her grand opening so far—

especially with the accounts receivable—and looked forward to Sunday morning. Since arriving in Brenham, she'd attended the second worship service with Uncle Jack and Kristi, allowing them to go on ahead of her for Bible study. She'd considered attending Sunday school but hadn't made the effort—a bit lazy on her part.

Sunday morning she managed to drag herself out of bed in time to leave with them. Morning was not her favorite time of the day, but she recognized she needed to give God priority on this issue.

All the way into town, Uncle Jack teased her about her lackadaisical manner and the coffee mug attached to her hand. "How did you manage early classes at school?" he asked.

"No problem," she replied. "If they were scheduled before ten, then I didn't take them."

"Someday motherhood will change your habits," Kristi said with a laugh. She reached over to plant a kiss on Walker's cheek. Already he had his mother's brown eyes and his daddy's dimples.

Cassidy took another sip of coffee. "No, they will be just like their mother and sleep very late."

When they drove into the church parking lot, Uncle Jack pulled in right beside Carlos. Handling Carlos so early in the morning might be a test of her faith, Cassidy thought. But a second glance revealed that he had a box of donuts. With her Bible and her new Carlos-crafted purse, she exited the car and pasted on a big smile.

"We meet again," Carlos said, leaning against the side of a spotless black truck. "Glad you're here. I think you'll like the group."

She shifted her shoulder purse. "I'm looking forward to making new friends."

They walked into the church together, and he escorted her to the room where the young adult class met. He introduced her to a young woman by the name of Tracey, a tall brunette

who served as the official greeter of the group.

"Would you keep Cassidy company and introduce her around while I check on some things?" Carlos asked.

She agreed, and he disappeared.

"I've seen you in church," Tracey said. "I should have welcomed you then."

"Well, I've met you now," Cassidy replied.

Tracey sorted through a stack of neatly piled papers from a nearby table. "First things first. How about completing a visitor's card for me?"

While Cassidy completed the visitor information, members slowly trickled into the large room. The smell of coffee permeated the area, and she needed another cup to manage the morning. One man sat down at the piano and began playing praise choruses. Tracey introduced Cassidy to many of the class members, and they all welcomed her warmly. Cassidy relaxed and selected a donut along with another cup of coffee. Between the caffeine and the sugared donut, she'd wake up and see what God had to say to her this morning.

Her mind swept back to her old church in New York where she'd left a dearly loved pastor. He had extraordinary insight into the Scriptures and always found time to spend with church members. Most Sunday services left her in tears, sometimes in joy and sometimes over her own sin. Pastor Greg Johnston at Brenham's Community Church did have excellent sermons, and she knew Jack counted him as a good friend. She needed to stop comparing the two pastors and simply concentrate on what Pastor Johnston had to say.

Cassidy had cherished her Sunday school class in New York, which was one reason she'd been reluctant to attend this one. The members had been closer than family—helping and praying for each other and simply enjoying the good company. They all knew she'd had a drug problem in high school and spent time in a recovery center, but the past didn't matter. They simply loved and accepted each other.

Sandwiched between Tracey and another girl, Cassidy drank her coffee and waited for the teacher to arrive.

"So what brought you to Brenham?" Tracey asked.

Cassidy lifted her gaze from her purse, where she'd been searching for a breath mint. "Oh, you can tell I'm not from around here?"

They laughed, and the humor set the pace for a more lively conversation.

"So, you're the owner of the new boutique, Cassidy's Charm?" Tracey asked. "I'll be sure to stop in."

"Thanks. I'm really proud of it. I want my shop to have fashionable clothes but at prices that don't inflate a woman's budget."

"My kind of place," Tracey replied. "Have you known Carlos long?"

"No, he's a friend of my uncle's, and he's also supplying my shop with leather belts, purses, and wallets."

"I didn't know he did leatherwork," Tracey said.

She showed her new friend the leather purse.

"Oh, it's gorgeous. Now, I must stop in." Tracey touched the delicate silver trim. "What brought you to little Brenham?"

"Jack Frazier is my uncle. When I graduated from college and indicated I'd like to open a boutique, he suggested I consider Brenham. So here I am, a long way from home but with loving family." She sighed and glanced down at her nearly empty Styrofoam cup. "God's been good to me. I'm not sure why He wants me in Texas, but I'm loving every minute of it. One problem though."

"What's that?"

"Everyone talks funny."

Once Tracey stopped laughing, she pointed to the front of the room. "Looks like we're ready to start the lesson. He's an awesome teacher."

Cassidy looked up, ready to give the teacher her full attention. Then her jaw dropped. Carlos Diaz stood up front.

Why am I not surprised? Cassidy asked herself. *Is there anything the man cannot do well? Talk about feeling inadequate. Here I am, ecstatic about obtaining a college degree and opening a business, and Mr. Perfect has his fingers dipping into everything.*

She tilted her head. Maybe perfectionists concentrated on organization and knew how to busy themselves with everything. Her dad had a lot of those same characteristics, and she loved him dearly, but he also drove her crazy with his nit-picky details for a disciplined life. Of course, it wouldn't hurt for her to pick up on a few of those traits.

"How many of you have experienced fear this month?" Carlos began. "This week? This morning? The kind of gut-wrenching fear that leaves you paralyzed, feeling powerless to do anything about your circumstances—and desperate enough to try anything." He paused. Cassidy noticed some heads nodding in understanding.

"We all have moments like that at one time or another," Carlos continued. "And we also face situations where someone we are close to strikes out at us because of such fear. In today's lesson, two men chosen by God are dealing with fear. The choices they make, both good and bad, contain lessons for all of us. Take your Bibles and turn to 1 Samuel 18:5–16."

Cassidy listened intently as Carlos described how King Saul's fear that David would claim his throne drove him to jealousy of the younger man. Tormented by fears of inadequacy and rejection by his own people, Saul tried many times to kill David. The king was so controlled by fear that he even damaged his relationship with his son Jonathan.

Cassidy clung to Carlos's every word. Saul's predicament reminded her of her own fears of being inadequate and how they fueled her sense of insecurity. She'd never felt quite good enough at anything she attempted. As a teen, she'd feared her mom and dad loved her younger, much more intelligent sister more than she. That fear turned to jealousy, and the jealousy

turned to rebellion—and the rebellion resulted in drug use. Those years in New York when she hadn't known God haunted her, filling her with guilt and shame. At times she felt so envious of Christians who had known Jesus since they were young children, especially when she compared their lives with the mess she'd made of hers.

Oh, God, I want my relationship with You to grow. Take away my guilt and the doubts I have about what You want to do with my life. I admit I'm afraid of why You want me here in Texas, but I want to follow You in obedience. Thank You for wonderful parents and a family who love me despite what I've done. And thanks for good men like Carlos. Help me not to be so critical of him and to offer friendship. In Jesus' name, amen.

four

Cassidy's Charm flourished over the next two weeks like a sprouting plant. Excitement poured from every inch of her. Each day brought surprises and usually a learning experience in dealing with the public. Her best talents lay in understanding how color, texture, and design worked together and then applying that information to the individual needs of her clients. Cassidy loved dressing each lady as if she were a model, regardless of the customer's age or size. The hours were long and grueling, but she enjoyed meeting so many women and thrived on assisting them select fashion-conscious apparel.

Kristi's mother, Paula Franklin, encouraged her guests from the Country Charm Bed and Breakfast to visit the boutique, and Cassidy decided to continue running an ad in the local newspaper, offering a discount on purchases. She welcomed each new day, even if it meant facing the arduous struggle to get up earlier in the morning.

"I have an idea," Cassidy said one evening while she helped Kristi bathe Walker. "At your mom and dad's B&B, hymns are piped throughout the house and outside around the gazebo. What about background contemporary Christian music at the boutique?"

"Sounds like a great idea to me," Kristi said, just as Walker decided to splash and soak his mother's face.

Cassidy handed her a towel. "I want something light, but not overpowering. I don't want anyone to think the shop caters to only teens or young adults."

"I bet Jack could put you in touch with someone to put in a sound system." Kristi lifted Walker to her shoulder. He had her

31

brown eyes and the Frazier blond hair. "Now, I have an idea, totally different from yours. Why not carve out a corner to put a few children's toys and books to entertain the toddlers while their mothers shop?"

Cassidy crossed her arms. "You are a wealth of ingenuity," she said. "I've had a few problems with children wanting to tear the place apart while their moms try on clothes."

Kristi tossed a lock of cocoa brown hair behind her shoulder and out of Walker's reach. "Badly behaved kids getting on your nerves? Believe me, motherhood has given me a whole new appreciation for well-disciplined children. I mean, I want Walker to be happy, but he will learn the rules."

Cassidy planted a kiss on the baby's cheek. "Do you want to help me pick out what I need? I'd like to set it up tomorrow."

Kristi laughed. "I can stop in after the baby's nap and bring a few toys and things."

Wrapping her arms around Kristi and the baby, Cassidy gave both a hug. "Don't know what I'd do without your advice and support," she said. "And you're so sweet to put up with me."

"You can stay here forever as far as we're concerned."

Cassidy felt tears pool in her eyes. "Thank you," she murmured. "Don't know what I've ever done to deserve this."

The following Sunday, Cassidy attended the young adult Sunday school class and met more people. A young man invited her to dinner, but she declined. Her life already held too many issues for her to want to complicate it with dating. She'd have plenty of time for social activities once the demands of her shop settled down.

Carlos's lesson was as relevant to everyday life as his previous talk had been. He confronted the dangers of sexual involvement outside marriage—and related temptations inherent in the contemporary dating scene—by discussing the mistakes David and Bathsheba made and the problems that resulted from their sin.

At the beginning of the worship service, Pastor Johnston made an announcement. "We have a little problem in the nursery this morning. Looks like we have more little ones than we anticipated and we need two people to volunteer as soon as possible. If any of you are so led, please exit to the rear where the director will lead you to the nursery."

Kristi reached for her purse, but Cassidy stopped her. "Let me go," she whispered. "You are busy with little Walker every day."

"Are you sure?" Kristi asked, glancing at her husband and back to Cassidy.

"Go ahead," Uncle Jack whispered, tucking Kristi's arm into his.

Cassidy slipped to the back and discovered Carlos waiting with the director. Did he busy himself with everything?

"Wonderful, we have our two volunteers," the elderly woman said once they shut the door to the sanctuary. "We need help with the babies."

"Walker's group?" Cassidy asked.

"Yes, he's in there, and oh, my, they are a handful today. All of them are crying and want their mamas."

Carlos chuckled. "Glad I have nieces and nephews, or I'd be lost."

The woman led them to the nursery, where a middle-aged woman told Carlos to carry each little one to a changing table where Cassidy could perform diaper duty.

"Do you think we were set up for this?" he whispered with a chuckle. "I envisioned us rocking little ones to sleep."

She muffled a laugh. "I think our fearless leader sniffed them all before we got here." His aftershave intoxicated her, a grand improvement over the odor emanating from the babies.

Twenty minutes later, all the babies smelled powder fresh, and most of them were happy. Cassidy had to laugh at Carlos's attempt to line up toys, books, diaper bags, and even children

according to size. Oddly enough, he never gave up, even when the woman in charge of the babies declared it impossible.

At the close of the hour, Cassidy sat on the floor with two lively babies and showed them how to place shapes into a hollow, plastic ball. She wanted to hold Walker, but Carlos had snatched him up and was reading from a cloth book about colors. He did do a good job with the babies, but she expected no less.

"How are you doing over there?" he asked from his perch on a rocking chair.

"Good," she replied, at last successful in urging a little girl to push in the properly shaped piece. "I'm playing teacher over here. Good thing I didn't follow through with my original intentions of teaching school."

"I already know my limitations," he replied. "But you're doing much better than I am. With my perfectionism, I'd want them to shove in those pieces on the first try." She heard the rocker squeak, and he joined her on the floor. "By the way, what were you going to teach?"

"High school English, but that went by the wayside for fashion merchandising."

"Interesting. English is where I have the hardest time, and I took Latin, Greek, and Hebrew in college. I may have to call on your expertise as I put together scholarship information."

She glanced at him strangely. The perfectionist wanted her help? Hadn't Uncle Jack said he'd received the Truman Scholarship? Must be a ploy to keep her in his Sunday school class. "Uh, sure. Just let me know."

Parents arrived for their babies in a flurry of activity. Carlos and Cassidy gathered up diaper bags and individual notes stating how each baby spent nursery time. They matched up security codes to ensure each little one went to the correct parent. Kristi and Jack took Walker, but other babies remained and the director needed to leave.

"I can take you home," Carlos offered Cassidy. "That way

Kristi and Jack won't have to wait with Walker." Just then Walker began to fuss. "See, he agrees with me."

"As long as you don't mind," Cassidy replied, and it was settled.

When all the children had finally been picked up, Carlos escorted her to his sleek black truck. She complimented him on its shiny finish.

"Thanks. I try to keep it looking good, but sometimes it's a challenge," he replied, opening the door for her.

"I guess that's one area where I am diligent," she said with a laugh. "I love my little yellow Bug."

"See, we have something in common," he said, sending chills to her toes with his smile.

The trip home passed comfortably with constant chatter about the morning, her shop, and his search for the right grad school.

Carlos appeared an enigma to her. Did the man ever sleep? She'd heard from Uncle Jack that Carlos worked with an evangelism team on Tuesday evenings along with helping out at the horse ranch six days a week ever since he'd graduated from college. She knew he'd been looking for a job more in line with his schooling, and when Cassidy inquired about his field of study, she learned he'd had a double major in history and economics. She felt tired just thinking about his expertise and daily schedule.

If she allowed herself to dwell on Carlos Diaz, her mind started to spin. His smile sent her heart racing, and as much as she denied it, she felt a pang of resentment when he shared his smiles with anyone else. Perhaps his good looks were all that attracted her, or his super intelligence, or the way he handcrafted leather, or the fact that her uncle Jack swore he had an innate ability to handle Arabian horses, or the way he taught Sunday school—or maybe his charm involved all those things.

But his obsession with perfectionism remained a trait

guaranteed to drive her nuts. She'd noted just that morning that before class he couldn't sit still until all the pencils in a box were stored with their points at the same end. Another time, the napkins beside the donuts were swirled instead of stacked in a neat pile, and he had to change them. Then there was his Bible: It had to rest directly on the corner of the podium where he taught his lesson. Cassidy almost giggled remembering how he refused to drink coffee before class because he didn't have a spoon to measure the creamer. Everyone else dumped in the white powder and mixed it with a plastic stirrer. Not Carlos.

She imagined his apartment must be as sterile as a hospital room and as neatly maintained as a librarian's desk. Did he ever relax? Prop up his feet on an end table? Wear a ragged T-shirt?

In any event, she didn't plan to clutter her mind with thoughts of him any longer. She had a business to run and goals to reach—none of which included Carlos Diaz.

five

The next week flew by, and on Friday Cassidy anchored her sites on Saturday night and a chance to breathe. The bell jingled and announced a customer.

"Good morning," Cassidy greeted. "Can I help you with something, or are you browsing?"

"Neither," the woman replied, and Cassidy's mind went momentarily blank.

"Okay," she finally replied and gestured toward the refreshment table. "We have cappuccino and fresh cookies—"

"I'm not interested."

The retort startled Cassidy. She moistened her lips while sending a quick prayer heaven's way. The woman looked a little older than her mother, but the harsh lines around her eyes and mouth detracted from any sense of pleasantness. Noting the stylish dress of her visitor, Cassidy thought she'd be attractive if a smile graced her lips.

"All right," Cassidy said, determined to be courteous, "I'm here if you need me."

"You, Missy, are the last thing on earth I need, which is why I'm here."

The woman's dagger-like response caught Cassidy unaware. "I beg your pardon. Have I offended you?"

"You're a disgrace to the retail industry." The woman stepped closer. Fire practically blazed from her eyes.

"I don't understand," Cassidy said. "You've just insulted me, and I'd like an explanation." She regretted that the one customer trying on several outfits must be hearing the impolite words.

"Your merchandise is marked considerably lower than

what is proper. In fact, it's vulgar."

"Vulgar? I believe a woman should be able to dress fashionably at an affordable price." Cassidy narrowed her gaze at the obnoxious woman.

"And I believe quality and cost go hand in hand."

The woman obviously owned a clothing store. "We have a difference of opinion," Cassidy said, willing her frazzled nerves to calm before she said something she'd regret. "And I have no intention of hiking my prices."

"You have cheapened brand names."

"I most certainly have not." Taking a deep breath, Cassidy plunged into what she hoped sounded like a mature response. "Apparently you own a shop, and my boutique has cut into your profits. I'm sorry for your misfortune, but I'm here to stay."

The woman glared angrily, tapping her foot against the hardwood floors. "I'm only warning you that the conscientious buyer will soon see you must carry inferior merchandise. Why else would it be cheaper?"

"Ma'am, I'm sorry you're angry, but this is a useless conversation. Maybe you'd better leave."

The woman opened her mouth to say more but abruptly closed it again. She headed toward the door, then shot back one last stinging comment over her shoulder. "We'll see who's still in business this time next year. No doubt, you will be bored by then with your little toy, while the rest of us hardworking people will be left to pick up the pieces."

Cassidy watched her leave. She trembled with the anger racing through her veins.

"Don't let her upset you," a voice behind her said. Cassidy turned to see the customer had emerged from the dressing room, carrying a stack of clothing articles. "She's afraid you'll run her out of business."

And she's jealous, Cassidy concluded. The memory of Carlos's first Sunday school lesson rolled through her mind.

"Thank you," Cassidy whispered and then smiled at the

customer. "I'll pray for her."

"That's all you can do, Honey, when bitter people attempt to take away your joy. You have the beginnings here of an excellent shop. Only a fool would fail to see your commitment to women and your love for the Lord."

Cassidy felt the tears pool in her eyes. Even if she was twenty-two years old, at that moment she could have used her mother's wise advice and comforting arms.

"I know the woman; her name is Thelma Myers," the customer continued, stepping forward and placing her hand on Cassidy's arm. "Her shop is overpriced, and she carries a lot of the same brands as you do here. Don't let her intimidate you."

Cassidy nodded and swallowed the emotion threatening to erupt. "I appreciate your kind words," she said.

The woman patted Cassidy's arm and handed her the stack of clothes. "Guess I should have finished sooner so she could have seen this stack of clothes I'm buying."

They laughed, and Cassidy snatched up a tissue to dab her eyes and aid her drippy nose. No sooner had the customer left, then Carlos walked in. He handed her a bag of foil-wrapped chocolates.

"Hi! I had some business in the neighborhood and thought you might need a chocolate fix." He glanced at her and frowned. "You look a little sad. Anything wrong?"

"Oh, I'm all right," she managed to say and flitted her gaze from one display to another while she regained her composure.

"Do you want to talk about it?"

He sounded sincere, and with the incident fresh on her mind and a willing listener, she almost unloaded everything, but Cassidy had always been one to keep her feelings to herself.

"Another shop owner doesn't care for me. Obviously she's concerned I will hurt her business. The confrontation reminded me of your Sunday school lesson, the one about fear leading to jealousy."

Carlos studied her intently. "Glad I'm getting through to somebody."

"Well, from the comments I hear on Sunday mornings, everyone believes you're a fantastic teacher," Cassidy added. "And I did pray for the shop owner while she complained."

"Good," he said, warmth radiating from his dark brown eyes. "This world is tough enough without adding resentment on top of all our other problems."

She nodded, and a burning ember of her former self crossed her mind. Resentment of her younger sister had nearly destroyed her, and guilt still tapped her on the shoulder. She bit back the tears, trying to forget.

Carlos broke the edge of silence. "If you take a lunch break, I'd ask you to join me," he said, arranging the paperclips on her counter.

"You're sweet, but I stay here during the noon hour. There is one thing you could do for me though," she said, hoping to mask the inescapable grief threatening to surface. "How about ripping into the bag of candy for me?"

"On one condition."

"What's that?"

"Go riding with me on Saturday evening after you get home from work. I have a full day to pull for Jack and will be finished about five."

She had mixed feelings about a date with him. Did he ever stop smiling? But how could she resist? "I haven't been riding in weeks. Sounds like fun."

"What about dinner afterwards?"

Startled, her gaze flew straight to his face. "I–I suppose," she replied.

Moments later, Carlos left the shop, leaving behind a bewildered Cassidy. While she'd concentrated on hiding her innermost thoughts, he'd asked her out and she'd accepted!

❧

All the way back to his apartment, Carlos wondered where

he'd left his brains. The last thing he needed was an incredibly tiny young woman with short tousled hair to add to his list of responsibilities. *But I'm simply her Sunday school teacher,* he told himself and immediately shoved Cassidy into a little corner of his Sunday morning.

He waited at a traffic light and a perky little blond crossed the street, reminding him of Cassidy once again. The owner of the newest boutique in Brenham had taken residence in his head, whether he liked it or not. The sound of her laughter and the way she took life easy held a strange attraction for him. He sensed a lot more depth to her than what she projected, and she certainly had a head for business.

Thinking about her counter at the shop, he shook his head. How could she live in such disorder? But somehow she managed, and the fact that her displayed items lay scattered about didn't bother her at all.

Maybe she'd be too tired on Saturday and decline the ride and dinner date. Whatever would he discuss with her? He doubted if the economic structure of Europe or the history of the Roman empire appealed to her. What a boring evening. He should kick himself.

Carlos turned into a drive-thru for lunch, grabbing a burger and fries, and toted them home in a greasy bag he placed carefully on top of a folded towel. Once in his apartment, he switched on his computer and set to work. In order to attend Harvard, he'd have to be awarded another scholarship or more financial aid. The deadline on most applications was January 31. Okay, first things first. He got online and read all the information about Harvard's scholarship programs for their school of government. Then he downloaded the various application forms.

He sighed and reached for one of the fries lined up like soldiers on his plate. They were cold. Wiping his fingers on a clean napkin, he sat back and deliberated on the grad school dilemma. If, by the grace of God, he received the extra funding

for Harvard, he'd be entering almost a year from now, like he'd planned. Patience had never been one of his finer points, and he'd have a long wait. If he didn't get the funds after building up his hopes for all the months leading up to the deadline, he'd be miserable. One thing was certain: He needed another job, one that utilized his studies and kept him on track for his career. He could still manage his responsibilities for Jack in the evenings and on Saturdays.

A thought occurred to him. He could apply to work for the city—a government position, which would look great on his résumé.

Finishing up his fries, he downed his drink and tossed the bag into the trash. Fearing the can might smell like food, he pulled out the plastic bag and replaced it.

He sighed. Might as well see what kind of jobs were out there. He brushed his teeth, changed his shirt, and snatched up his keys.

six

Cassidy's Saturday afternoon zipped by with a flurry of customers and all the headaches involved in maintaining a retail business. Labor Day weekend traditionally brought out many shoppers, but she hadn't expected it to be this wild. She loved every aspect of her job except for the unruly children, and thankfully the new tot's corner helped tremendously in resolving that problem. She hadn't had time to eat lunch, so when she put up the "closed" sign and locked the door of Cassidy's Charm at 5:10, she felt slightly weak and sensed the low rumble of a demanding stomach. She turned back to the refreshment table and snatched up two cookies, then finished the rest of the cappuccino, determined to eat a decent dinner later that evening.

That's when she remembered her plans with Carlos.

"I must have been out of my mind to accept a date with him," she said aloud. As tired as her body felt, she expected his perfectionism would drive her nuts. Granted, it had been a long time since she'd actually spent time with a guy, but that didn't mean she had to subject herself to an evening of eccentric and bizarre behavior.

Suddenly she realized her narrow-minded evaluation of him wasn't fair or Christ-like. To be honest, Carlos had a likeable side, which she had noted from the beginning. His close walk with the Lord and his commitment to teaching young-adult Sunday school said a lot about his character. And if she permitted it, those rich, dark eyes and broad shoulders coupled with his incredible smile could set her heart into a whirl. But she wouldn't allow such feelings. Friendship is what she needed now. Too many goals took priority at this stage of her

life to risk becoming involved with anyone.

Stop it, Cassidy. Get a grip, and don't think of anything but why you're in Texas.

Popping the rest of a white chocolate macadamia nut cookie into her mouth, she proceeded to sweep up crumbs around the refreshment table. Next she stuffed the contents of the cash register drawer into a bank envelope, then headed for home.

The afternoon had been gorgeous—lots of sun without the sweltering temperatures that had attacked her body earlier in the summer. Bright colored geraniums, impatiens, and hibiscus bloomed as though it were mid-summer. What a shock to her senses, although she never liked driving in snow and ice anyway. By this time in New York, she'd have pulled out some sweaters and jackets to wear on the occasional nippy evening. With a shrug, she decided that living in Texas, half her winter clothes would hang idle in her closet.

Maneuvering her little yellow Bug into the circular driveway of Jack and Kristi's Victorian-style home, Cassidy instantly spotted Carlos near the barn. Her pulse quickened and a sweet little tingle raced up and down her spine. The sensation unnerved her. Quickly she chased away any romantic notions. She intended to ride a horse and fill up the empty spot in her stomach. Period.

Stepping from her car, she heard Uncle Jack call her name. She turned and waved; naturally Carlos smiled so broadly she had the same stupid reaction again—a reaction that was beginning to annoy her. Too bad feigning a headache fell under the heading of dishonesty.

Inside the tastefully decorated home, a mixture of French country and antiques, Kristi and Walker were involved in dinner—rather Walker wanted to eat and his mommy couldn't shovel the food in fast enough. Cassidy giggled at the way he cried between bites.

"Eats like his daddy," Kristi said with a laugh, scraping the

sides of a nearly empty jar of baby food, then snatching up another one full of green beans. "You'd think he hadn't eaten all day."

"You're the comical one," Cassidy remarked, observing the two. "Every time you bring the spoon to his mouth, you open yours."

Kristi frowned and pressed her lips together in an obvious attempt to keep from laughing. "Jack and Mom accuse me of the same thing. Say. . ." She glanced up into Cassidy's face. "I hear you and Carlos are going riding and then having dinner."

Cassidy averted her gaze. "News travels fast."

"Don't you want to go?"

"I'm not sure," she replied. "One minute I do, and the next I don't."

"So, what's the problem?" Kristi grabbed a wet washcloth and wiped a smudge of green from Walker's chin.

"A whole bunch of things—wondering if this is what I'm supposed to do. You know, start a relationship with a guy when I need to be concentrating on my business."

"Friendships are necessary for living," Kristi said, pulling a piece of baby food from her thick hair. "And those are my words of wisdom for the day."

Cassidy laughed at her comment. Still a nagging thought refused to leave her alone. "Kristi, does Carlos know about. . . you know, what I did to Uncle Jack?"

Kristi paused until Walker protested. Filling his spoon she took a deep breath. "Sweetie, you're harboring old stuff, but Carlos did work here when Jack first moved to Brenham. They've always been good friends, so I'm assuming he knows. But Jack has forgiven and forgotten all about those days, and you should, too."

Cassidy reached down to remove her shoes. "I can't, not just yet. It's always foremost in my mind, along with how irresponsibly I acted toward my family."

Kristi turned to her. "God forgave you and so has everyone

who loves you. You need to stop punishing yourself and simply be His little girl."

Sighing, Cassidy picked up her heeled shoes. "I understand," she said, but the heaviness still weighed down her heart. "If you don't need me for anything, I'm going to change."

"No, go right ahead. And remember, I'm praying for you."

Cassidy kissed the top of Walker's head, one of the few spots not covered by the disgusting green vegetables. "Thanks. I'm working on it, too."

Once she wiggled into her boots and jeans and pulled on a T-shirt that said "I Love New York," she strolled to the barn, masking her reservations with a determination to enjoy the evening.

❦

When Carlos saw Cassidy strolling his way, his heart did a double somersault. This wasn't supposed to happen. He'd regretted his invitation the moment he'd asked her, and now his senses decided to play a game of betrayal. No, not Carlos. He had no intentions of getting involved with a half-pint blond who drove him crazy with her lack of organization. His goals for the future, the things he knew for certain God had outlined for him, didn't include any woman yet. And when the time came, it wouldn't be a woman like Cassidy Frazier. He needed more than a pretty face for a future wife. He needed a friend and companion who shared his interests and tastes. Her kitchen cupboards would be as organized as his office.

What am I thinking? This is a one-time-only horseback ride across the fields, followed by dinner in Brenham.

"Why are you so pale?" Jack asked as he dismounted Desert Wind. "Are you sick?"

Carlos tossed him a bewildered stare. "No, I feel perfectly fine."

"Well, you don't look so fine to me," Jack said, then chuckled as he led the horse inside the stable.

Carlos touched his forehead. He did feel warm; but he'd been working.

"Hi," Cassidy called. "Do you still want to go riding?"

"Sure. I just need to saddle us a couple of horses." He wondered why he hadn't noticed her slender figure before. Of course, she hadn't been wearing jeans at the shop.

"I can saddle my own. It'll be faster," she replied. "Hi, Uncle Jack. Did you get a new transmission for Kristi's car?"

"Yeah, but I had the garage do the work, although the warranty had expired. You're busy enough without doing car repairs," Jack replied.

Carlos stared at her oddly. "You fix cars?"

She tossed him a beaming smile. "It's a hobby. I figure if I can't make it in the fashion retailing business, I can always be a mechanic." She peered around the corner to where Jack was busy brushing Desert Wind. "I'd looked forward to the work. Help me pay my room and board."

"I'd rather you baby-sit than get grease under your manicured nails," Jack said. "Hard to sell all that frilly stuff with dirty hands."

She wrinkled her nose at him and grabbed a bridle. Carlos filed the information into his brain as a digest-later item. Somehow he couldn't picture her underneath a car hood in dirty coveralls.

A short while later, Carlos and Cassidy trotted across a field bordering on a narrow creek. They rode newly broken mares, and the horses wanted to run.

"Shall we give them their heads?" Cassidy asked with a daring tone in her voice. "I'd like to race."

"Can you handle her?" Carlos replied. "She's pretty frisky."

"Uncle Jack taught me to ride before I enrolled in kindergarten. Are you afraid I'll outdo you?"

He sunk his heels into his mare's sides, managing to speed ahead of her. "To the live oak," he called as he passed by. "The one by the creek."

She held her own, and he thought for a moment she might beat him, but she didn't.

"You had a head start," she said, once they stopped beneath the spreading branches of the tree.

"I'd rather call it a definite advantage," he said, noting the flush of pink in her cheeks and way the wind tossed her short blond curls.

"Where I come from, it's called cheating," she flung at him with a toss of her head.

"Here, it's simply a case of the best horse." He chuckled. "Do Yankees hate to lose?"

"Absolutely." She laughed, and this time he caught the flash of a twinkle in her eyes.

"Would you like to walk along the creek?" he asked. "This breeze feels good after the hot day I've put in."

They dismounted and led their horses along the shady bank. With the close of the afternoon settling about them, the sun sparkled off the creek, magical and teasing. They stood silently watching the shimmering water.

"What a lovely place," she finally said. "It's peaceful, and I'm always for a little serenity."

He nodded. "It's too easy to get caught up in the whirlwind of life and forget what God's given us to enjoy."

"Are you being philosophical?" she asked, her soft teasing voice swirling around his senses.

"Probably." He couldn't help but smile.

"So are you going to be a philosopher or a politician?"

"Both, like you and the mechanics business." He stared at her curiously. "How did you ever take up car repair?"

"Well," she began and sadness spread across her face, "in high school, I did some pretty wild things." She glanced at him guardedly. "You already know about my past problem with drugs, don't you?"

"Yes," he said. "Jack and I became friends shortly after he moved here. You don't have to talk about anything that

makes you feel uncomfortable."

Her blue gray eyes relayed her appreciation. "Thanks, but it's all right, really." She stared out over the water and a crow called. "While in drug rehab, we were instructed to pick up a life class, something we could utilize when we were free again." She patted her horse. "Rebellion happened to be my middle name, so I decided if I had to be there, then I would select something I would never use."

"Car mechanics," he whispered.

"Right. The funny part is that I like it, and I'm good at fixing things." She tossed a grin in his direction. "I know I don't look like a grease monkey, but there are stranger things in this world."

"I know just enough about cars to scare me," he said. "Maybe you can teach me a few things. Beyond oil changes, changing tires, and replacing batteries and belts, I'm lost."

"Can't imagine me teaching you anything. From all I've heard, you're the brilliant one."

He felt his face warm. "Not exactly. I study hard."

"Hmm, graduated with honors from A&M in three years. Sounds impressive to me. Looks like great things in your future."

"Like what?" he asked, enjoying their light-hearted conversation.

She placed her finger on her chin. "Governor Diaz. . . Congressman Diaz. . .Senator Diaz. . .President Diaz. Some day I'll be able to say I let Carlos Diaz beat me in a horse race."

"You let me?" he questioned with feigned annoyance.

A pained expression instantly clouded her face. Her gaze flew to the ground, and he saw she stood in a bed of ants.

Cassidy jumped from the pile. "What are these?" she asked, stomping her feet. "They're stinging me."

seven

"Fire ants," Carlos replied. "Let me help you get those boots off."

She winced. She lowered her eyebrows and wrinkled the bridge across her nose. "Ouch. There must be a million of those things biting me."

"I'm sure it feels like that." He took her mare's reins and tied both horses to the trunk of a sapling. Kneeling on the grass, he reached for her boot. Two ants crawled up his hand.

"Carlos, they'll bite you. I'll get my boots."

"I think I can handle a few fire ants," he said, shaking them away. "Sit down and let me do the chivalry thing." He tugged on one boot, gave it a fling, and yanked off the other one.

She pulled off her socks to find several ants had inched their way down the top of her foot. With a swipe she sent a number of them flying.

"Get going, you nasty things," she said, wiggling her toes. Peering up at him through watery eyes, she dampened her lips. "My feet and lower legs are on fire," she said, rubbing the rapidly swelling area. "This must be how they got their name."

He sighed, hating her discomfort and feeling helpless in its wake. "Probably so. My mother would bring out the seasoned salt and make a paste for where they bit you," he said. "I believe the tenderizing agent pulls out the sting."

Cassidy pursed her lips. "We're a good mile from Kristi's pantry. Got any more ideas?"

"Acupuncture?" he replied with a grin. "Or I could tell you a story like I do my nieces and nephews."

"If it doesn't stop hurting, I may try both," she said, examining the inflamed red spots covering her feet and lower legs.

"I know what I can do," she said, lifting her head in the direction of the creek. "I'm going wading."

Carlos sat back on his heels. "I'm not so sure creek water has medicinal properties."

"Maybe not, but I'm in no mood to simply sit and endure the pain." She stood and hobbled toward the water. "Come on and join me." She beckoned toward the creek.

"Oh, I'll watch," Carlos replied, mentally calculating when he'd planned to have dinner and what this interruption would do to his schedule.

"I bet you forgot to enter a potential fire ant problem into your planner," she called. "And now we'll run behind."

He hurried behind her, cringing at the truth in her words. "No, Miss Frazier. My feet are smelly." Which they were.

"Who cares? Mine are red and swollen. In fact, the bites are the same color as my toe polish," she replied, bending to roll up the legs of her jeans to her calves. She stepped into the water. "Oh, this is wonderful. I bet you can't swim." Her mischievous look challenged him.

"I think you've just insulted my male integrity. But I do have to warn you about something."

She dipped her hand into the water and sent a handful spraying to his face. "What's that? Sharks in them there waters?" She attempted a southern drawl.

"No, Ma'am," he replied, mocking her attempt at Texas culture. "Snakes."

Her eyes widened and suddenly she appeared to dance on her toes in her haste to exit the creek. "You'd better be teasing me," she shouted. "I don't need snakes and fire ants in one day."

By the time she stepped onto the ground, her head was bobbing about like a chicken, apparently looking for anything crawling.

"I'm teasing," he said, feeling slightly ashamed of scaring her. "Well, maybe a little. There are snakes around here. You just have to be cautious and prepared for them."

"Prepared? Are you kidding?" she asked and swallowed hard.

He reached for her hand in an attempt to soothe her anxiousness, but the soft touch sent a tingling sensation through him again. He wanted to jerk it back but couldn't, given her uneasiness about his teasing. He knew the ant bites had to be smarting.

"Let's simply relax a moment," he said. "Have a seat and I promise not to give you a bad time."

She studied the ground.

"No strange creatures," he said, sitting on a grassy spot and gently urging her to do the same.

"All right," she muttered. The look she gave him warned him she would brook no more teasing. She eased down beside him, entirely too close for his comfort or good judgment. The scent of raspberry wafted around her.

"I'm sorry," he said.

"No, you're not," she replied curtly. "I think you've enjoyed every moment of giving this city girl the business." A slow smile spread over her face. "I'd have probably done the same thing, given the chance."

"So you won't let the water out of my radiator?" he asked, unable to tear his gaze away from her face. In a moment's glance, he'd memorized a tiny scar above the right corner of her lip, her thick veil of lashes, and a smudge of eye shadow no doubt from her slightly tearful encounter with the ants.

She tossed her attention back to the horses. "I might cut your girth." Her stomach growled and she shut her eyes. "I'm starved," she said. "Where are we eating tonight?"

"A little steakhouse on the north side of town."

"What's the dress?"

He pointed to her bare feet with the berry colored toe polish. "Shoes are required."

She shook her head then lifted her face to a ray of sunshine filtering through the tree limbs. "I wish we'd packed sandwiches."

"Well, let's get you back and dressed for dinner. I certainly don't want a rumor going around the Sunday school class that I tortured and starved you to death."

"Your next lesson could be on the Good Samaritan."

He agreed and helped her to her feet. She stared at him oddly. "You aren't wearing a hat," she noted.

"Nope, only in the daytime to fight off the sun."

"A purpose for the perfectionist," she said. "What about a baseball cap?"

"Yes, I have a few."

"Which way do you wear it?" she asked.

He had no idea what she was talking about. "Like everyone else," he replied.

"My point," she replied, snatching up her boots and socks and limping toward the horses.

Confused, he called after her, "I don't get it."

"You're not supposed to." She whirled around to face him. "Carlos, you're a great guy, but you need to come out of your box. Wade in a creek. Be late for an appointment. And," she tossed him a wide grin, "wear your cap backwards."

If any other woman had made such a declaration, he'd have shrugged it off and gone about his business. Hadn't his mother asked him to get out of his box? But for some reason, the comment coming from Cassidy made him want to tear at a corner of his little self-contained world.

☙

Cassidy brushed mascara over her lashes for the second time. Between the hunger pangs and the ant bites, she'd just as soon devour a peanut butter and honey sandwich and crawl into bed. Kristi had given her ointment to apply to the festering spots on her feet and legs, but the medication needed more time to work. To make matters worse, the ointment smelled horrible. She grabbed a washcloth and wiped it off. She could deal with the prickly-like discomfort but not the smell. She added a squirt of raspberry body spray and winced

as the alcohol stung her feet.

Scrutinizing her outfit in the mirror, she wondered if the skirt looked a bit too short. In fact, it did; plus the length allowed the ant bites to stick out rather conspicuously. Stepping out of the garment, she tossed it onto her bed along with a mound of other discarded outfits for the evening. A quick look at the clock caused her to cringe. Carlos would be waiting. Grabbing a pair of black slacks, a turquoise short-sleeved sweater, and matching jewelry, she vowed not to change again.

She ran her fingers through damp hair and shook her head to let the pesky natural curls fall where they may. Sliding lipstick around her mouth, she once again thought about the comforts of a bed. She'd gone to a lot of trouble for her first and last date with Carlos Diaz.

ﾞ

Carlos observed Cassidy while he pretended to study the menu. Their conversation had been sparse since she'd descended the stairs at Jack's and announced she was ready. He wondered what had happened to upset her between their conversation at the creek bank and when they'd headed off for dinner. The Cassidy he'd come to know always had something to say.

He'd complimented the way she looked, especially the bluish green shade of her sweater and the way it deepened her blue gray eyes. In fact, she'd nearly taken his breath away.

"We're not talking much," he said, setting down the menu.

She glanced up. "I'm sorry. Guess I'm tired."

"What about those ant bites?"

She tilted her head. "Oh, they're better. Thanks."

A moment later the waitress arrived with their water. They gave her their orders, and he asked for a basket of warm bread.

"Thanks," she whispered leaning across the table. "I love bread with lots of butter."

"As much as chocolate?" he asked, hoping the question would bring about a smile.

"Almost." Her lips turned upward.

He decided to brave a topic of interest, something more intellectual. After all, the dim lighting and a beautiful woman required stimulating conversation. What should it be—world affairs, politics, economic conditions in the U.S., the spread of evangelism in underdeveloped countries? But every time he opened his mouth, he forgot what he intended to say. This would never do for the man who earnestly desired a career in politics.

Lord, guide my words and help me say the right things. If this is my only date with Cassidy, I need to at least strive for an intelligent and meaningful conversation.

"I appreciate your contributions to the Sunday school class," he said. "Most new members avoid participating until they are better acquainted with the others."

"Your teaching makes it easy," she said and looked up as the waitress set a cloth-covered basket on the table along with two plates and butter. Cassidy lifted the cloth and pulled out a roll. Her eyes sparkled the way he remembered them near the creek. "These *are* warm," she said, obviously pleased.

"Good. I'd hate for you to wither up and blow away. Cassidy, I know very little about you," he said. "You're a long way from home and in a little town that doesn't have a whole lot to offer, at least not like New York."

She tore off a piece of the bread and popped it into her mouth. She chewed it slowly as though contemplating her answer. "God led me here for some reason, possibly to fulfill my goals."

"For your boutique?"

"Yes, and to work through a few issues about what He wants me to do with my life." She tore off another piece of bread and stared at it for a moment. "Carlos, I hate the fact that you know what I did in my teen years."

"You shouldn't. Doesn't make any difference to me. Friends aren't supposed to harbor feelings about the past. After all, God doesn't."

He knew the story about Cassidy from Jack. She'd been a rebellious girl caught up with divorcing parents and no thought of God. She'd turned to drugs, but Jack had found out. When he tried to help, she claimed he'd tried to molest her. Jack had gone to jail for six months, until a friend of Cassidy's revealed the truth. Although the court had overturned his conviction, Jack's brother, Rand, made life miserable until Jack left the state to start all over again in Texas. Rand refused to believe in his brother's innocence or his daughter's use of drugs until much later.

"But you know what I did. It still bothers me."

"What's important is you found the Lord."

She offered a sad smile. "Yes, Dad and I both did when I spent those weeks in the rehabilitation center."

He remembered the rest of the story. After Cassidy and Rand accepted the Lord into their lives, Rand traveled to Texas to mend his and Jack's strained relationship. He'd succeeded. When Jack and Kristi were married, Cassidy served as maid-of-honor.

"God used those circumstances for a lot of good, just like the Bible says," Carlos pointed out.

"You're right," she said. "I'm praying about it constantly. Have you ever wondered why God forgives and forgets, but we go on remembering it all?"

Carlos cleared his throat. "I think those feelings fall under the heading of guilt and shame, and God doesn't want those things haunting us."

"I know and I understand." She paused. "Thanks for being my friend," she said. "I really don't want to talk about this anymore." She finished her roll, and Carlos grappled for another topic, but before he could say a word, she had changed her pensive mood to all smiles.

"Will you tell me about your job for Uncle Jack?" she asked.

Carlos realized Cassidy Frazier needed his prayers. He'd been very wrong about her. All this time he'd thought she'd moved to Brenham on a whim—possibly spending a bit of her daddy's money out of boredom. Not so, he surmised. Guilt about the past had thrown her into a tailspin. Perhaps she thought if Jack had found God's peace in Brenham, she might be able to drop her heavy baggage right here, too. How long before she realized God lived in her heart, not in a small town in Texas?

He glanced at her angelic face and took a breath of the raspberry scent encircling her. Growing closer to Cassidy could do irreparable damage to his heart, certainly something far from what he believed God had planned.

eight

Carlos hung up the phone and shot his fist into the air. *"Whoooop!"* he shouted, using the Aggie A&M yell. He'd gotten the job with the Brenham Housing Authority, and they wanted to see him that afternoon.

"Thank You, Lord," he added, too excited to do anything but pace across the room. At last, after graduating summa cum laude at A&M, he could utilize some of his studies and interests. Of course he could have taken a job in Houston or Dallas over two months ago when he received his diploma, but that would have left his mother fending for herself and Jack without a trainer. So why had he gone and applied for entrance into Harvard's grad school program? Sometimes his plan of action made no sense to him at all.

The city position involved helping low-income people qualify for government-subsidized housing. He would help them complete their applications, then work closely with each applicant until they were placed into a suitable home or apartment. He knew his ethnicity and success in college had helped him land the job, but his willingness and desire would build his credibility. He sighed and puffed out his chest. This would look great on his résumé. He had to tell someone or he'd bust.

After a call to his mother, he calmed down slightly. He wanted to tell Cassidy but hadn't talked to her except at church since they'd gone out over four weeks ago. His reaction to her on their date had turned his heart and mind upside down, and seeing her in Sunday school confirmed his suspicions—spending much time with Cassidy Frazier invited problems with his future. The twinges at his heart were a consistent warning to

him. She merely wanted a friend, but he could all too easily fall in love.

A smart man would keep his distance.

He thought back over the Sunday school class activities. They'd held a luncheon, and he'd noted Cassidy contributed a lot to the group. He'd asked for volunteers to visit potential members on Tuesday evangelism nights, and she'd showed up when none of the others had time. He admired her more than he cared to admit.

Friends are for sharing, he reasoned. And what kind of friend would he be if he didn't tell her the news? Snatching up his baseball cap and keys, he decided to make a quick visit to Cassidy's Charm. As his palm touched the doorknob, he remembered something she'd said. He turned the brim of his cap around to the back. If she noticed his little idiosyncrasies, then others did too.

He found a little boost in his walk as he headed toward his truck. Funny how good news could lift a person's spirit. Anticipation nudged him to go faster. This had everything to do with his new job and nothing to do with seeing Cassidy, he assured himself.

On the way downtown, Carlos felt his brakes grab at a light. He'd have to drive by the car dealership to have them checked out after visiting Cassidy.

"Great," he muttered aloud, when he realized his warranty had expired. He should have purchased the extended service contract when he'd bought the truck, but back then he hated to spend the extra money.

🙠

Cassidy arranged the display of leather purses over a draping of brown velvet cloth and fall leaves. She'd sold three on Saturday and had orders for six more. That didn't leave her much choice but to call Carlos. She wanted to see him, other than in front of a Sunday school class, but her better judgment attempted to jostle the thought from her mind. It didn't

work. All of her grandiose ideas about a simple friendship sounded perfect until she caught a glimpse of him on Sunday mornings.

She appreciated his good looks, but his heart for others attracted her the most. One Sunday morning a young man requested prayer as he fought an addiction to alcohol. Not only did Carlos ask for volunteers to remember their classmate during the week, but he also stopped the lesson so that all of them could pray right then. Another time, a member's mother needed transportation to·M. D. Anderson Cancer Center in Houston for treatments. Carlos organized a car pool along with a prayer chain.

Watching him mirror Jesus inspired her to live a more loving Christian life. She began rising a little earlier in the mornings to resume a quiet time and, as a result, found her day more peaceful. But no matter how determined she was to keep Carlos at a distance, she found herself falling for him by merely being in the same room. *Love by osmosis,* she thought. *This is bizarre.*

Soon customers began dropping by her shop, and she shoved Carlos Diaz and any thoughts about him to the most remote part of her heart.

Around eleven-thirty, the bell jingled above the door and Carlos stood in the doorway. She smiled and waved, her heart turning cartwheels, especially when she saw he wore his cap backwards.

"I'll be right with you," she said from the dressing-room area. "I have a customer."

"Do you want me to come back later?" he asked, his voice sending sweet tremors up her spine.

"No," she replied much too quickly. She struggled to rein in her over-exuberance at seeing him. "I need to order more purses," she said more calmly.

As she assisted her customer in putting together three outfits to mix and match, Cassidy felt as though Carlos was

watching her. But whenever she managed to sneak a peek his way, he seemed intent on studying the purse display. Hopefully he hadn't decided to rearrange it.

Once the customer paid for her purchases and left, Cassidy felt awkward, like a child caught with her hand in the cookie jar. She hadn't been alone with Carlos since their date a month ago.

"Hi," he said, sounding a bit shy. "So you need more purses?"

"Yes. The ladies go wild over them. I wrote a check for you this morning." She opened the cash register and eased out a drawer where she'd placed it. "Looks like both of us are doing well in this arrangement."

"Thanks," he said, taking a quick look before folding the check. "How are you doing?"

"Good. Busy. What about you?" She wanted to ask why he hadn't called. Friends did keep up with each other. "I like your cap."

He smiled, easily coaxing a return grin from her. "I'm working on rounding out the corners of my box." He chuckled. "I have a bit of news. I got the job for the city, the one I told you about."

"Wonderful. I know you must be thrilled. Have you started yet?"

"Tomorrow. I'm supposed to stop in this afternoon for the paperwork."

"Do you have time to tell me about it?" she asked. For the next few minutes, Carlos explained the position with the city of Brenham. He sounded sincere in wanting to help families better themselves.

"I've always had a comfortable home and all my needs met plus more," she said. "How sad to want to provide for your family and not be financially able. I really admire what you're doing."

"Hopefully I can make a difference." He glanced at his

watch. "I need to get going. Got to have my brakes checked before my appointment."

"Slipping?" she asked. "I thought when I rode in your truck that they grabbed a little. Guess I should have mentioned it then." She peered outside. "Are you parked close by?"

"Right down the street."

"Can I take a look? I want to see if your rotors are warped."

"Be my guest," he said and gestured toward the front door.

Soon afterward she brushed the dirt from her hands. "Your rotors are warped, which means you need a brake job."

His brows narrowed. "Not the best news of the day."

"Let me do it for you," she said. "It will only take about an hour or so, and I work for free."

He shook his head. "I don't know."

"I fixed Uncle Jack's when I first got here. Talk to him if you doubt my capabilities."

A wry grin formed on his handsome face. "I don't doubt your abilities. I just hate for you to get your hands dirty at a man's job."

"They clean up just fine. I have this special goop that makes them soft and removes all the dirt." She tilted her head, unable to resist teasing him. "Do I hear a bit of male ego here? Does a lady mechanic strike a bad nerve?"

He stuffed his hands in his jeans pockets. "You win, but I want to pay you."

"This one's on me. I might let you assist me, though."

They made arrangements for her to repair his brakes after work. She had the necessary tools, but he needed to pick up the new parts from an auto store. Cassidy refused to think about the dangers of spending time alone with him. She was a smart girl—smart enough to keep her emotions in check.

❧

"I still don't like the idea of a woman replacing my brakes," Carlos repeated. He admired how adorable she looked wearing his cap backwards and sporting coveralls the size of a

child's. "This makes me feel like a wimp."

"Don't worry about it," Cassidy replied, rummaging through her toolbox. "Who knows? I might need political favors one day."

He scowled and she laughed. "I believe those are illegal." He eyed her up and down. "I admit you're the best looking mechanic I've ever seen. Guys don't fill out the coveralls like you do."

She wagged a ratchet in front of his face. "Better watch the teasing until I'm finished. I'd hate to see you sail through a stop sign because of bad brakes."

"Okay, okay. But I'm buying dinner when you're finished."

"You don't have to." She nibbled on her lip and the familiar sparkle of her blue gray eyes captured his attention. "Since we have a role reversal here, why don't you cook for both of us?"

"Men cook," he said, "and I do a great job."

"Good, it's a deal. I bet Kristi will let you use her kitchen while I'm cleaning up."

Carlos insisted upon jacking up the truck. At least he could do something. The thought of taking notes occurred to him, but he tossed the idea aside when he considered how ridiculous it would look.

He watched her lay out the tools like a doctor preparing for surgery. She amused him, and he soon realized she'd been trained well. Her small hands removed a wheel, which weighed a little less than she did, and pushed it aside. Naturally she refused his help. Carlos quickly gathered up the lug nuts and placed them side-by-side in a nice even row.

"The first thing I'm going to do is bleed the brake line," she said and tossed him a grin. "Is this hard for your perfectionism?"

"For certain," he replied. "It's killing me."

"I suppose you can organize my toolbox while you're waiting."

"Oh, I'm good at organization." He grinned. "So what are

you going to do next?"

"Make sure there is pressure on the caliper before I open it up and remove the old brake pads."

Carlos watched her work. She replaced the wheel bearings, rotors, and brake pads, lubed the caliper slide so the brake pads wouldn't stick on the rotors, and tested the new brakes. A few things he didn't understand, but pride stopped him from asking for clarification.

"Done," she sang out a while later, wiping off her tools on a rag and handing them to him. He carefully placed each one into the toolbox. "And boy, did I save you money." She peered up at him. "What's for dinner? Peanut butter and jelly? Grilled cheese? Hot dogs?"

"We're going out," he said and crossed his arms over his chest. "I don't want to bother Kristi when she has her hands full with Walker and Jack, and we can go somewhere super casual."

"Are you sure? I didn't do this brake job to weasel a dinner invitation."

"I know, but I think it's high time we had a little talk."

nine

Cassidy's emotions teetered between anger and confusion. She'd saved Carlos a ton of money by doing his brake job, and he acted as though she'd done something inappropriate. Pressing her lips together, she glared up at him.

"Hold on," he said, defending himself with his hands. "Hear me out before you think the worst of me." He took one of her grease-laden hands in his. "I want to show you how much I appreciate what you've done. I'm being selfish, but I want you all to myself without any interruptions."

She met his gaze, and although she knew the dangers of drowning in his dark eyes, she dared not refuse one glimpse of the face that had haunted her for weeks.

He reached up and brushed a finger over the tip of her nose. "Grease," he whispered, "but you wear it well." A light smile tugged at the corners of his mouth, and he continued in the same soft tone. "So what do you say?"

She felt the words crawl up her throat and camp there. She nodded her agreement. Carlos stood dangerously close, and she felt herself trembling. The sensation disturbed her. She'd always been the one in charge with men, but none of them had affected her like Carlos.

"I–I need to get cleaned up," she managed to stammer, feeling a sudden surge of warmth rising from the neck of her coveralls.

"I see another dirt spot." He leaned closer, a breath away from her mouth. "Right here." And his lips brushed across hers claiming a light kiss. His smile stretched across his handsome features. "You are beautiful."

While a million clever responses used to dance across her

mind when presented with a compliment, none leaped to her rescue now.

Help me, Lord. "I think you must be overwhelmed by my brake job," she said, feeling utterly foolish.

"Don't think so," he said, taking a step back and still wearing his unforgettable smile. "I think I'm captured by Cassidy's charm—and," he paused as he stooped to pick up a clamp, "it has nothing to do with a fashion boutique."

With renewed determination not to look like an idiot any longer than she already had, Cassidy snatched up a rag to wipe the dirt and grease from her hands. "Guess I'll tidy up and get showered," she said. "I'll hurry."

He snapped her toolbox shut. "I'll take care of this. In fact, I'm going to run into town and change clothes. I should be back about the same time you're finished."

She took a deep breath and mumbled "thanks" before setting her sights on the house.

"Do I need to apologize?" he asked.

She swung her gaze over her shoulder. "No, not at all."

Quickening her walk, she sensed her legs turning to jelly. What on earth had happened to her? She'd been kissed before, but certainly no other kiss had produced such a reaction. This wasn't the time to fall for a guy; she had too many other things to consider. Relationships were for the future, after she'd proven to her family their trust in her hadn't been wasted.

Inside, Kristi busied herself with dinner preparations. The spicy scent of chili floated around the kitchen while Walker used a wooden spoon to beat out a rhythm on the bottom of a pan.

"Hungry?" Kristi asked above the clatter.

"Yes, I'm starved, but Carlos wants to take me out."

Kristi turned from the stove to speak, but her expression quickly changed to alarm. "Cass, are you all right? Did you get overheated in those coveralls? Your face is redder than my chili."

Cassidy ducked around the corner to the staircase leading to her room. "No, I'm fine," she replied.

"I don't want you getting sick," Kristi said. She paused. "Unless Carlos put the color in your face. By the way, have you noticed his adorable dimple?"

Cassidy refused to answer. What good would it do?

❧

"Gotta minute?" Jack asked, while Carlos finished putting away Cassidy's tools inside her Bug's trunk.

Jack stared at him; his lips pursed and his eyebrows narrowed.

"It's Cassidy, isn't it?" Carlos asked, feeling the anger simmer through his veins. "You saw me kiss her, and now you don't want me dating her."

Jack waded his fingers through his blond hair. "You know better than that. You're like a brother to me. My concern is for both you and my niece—her emotions in particular."

"Go on," Carlos said, "you think I'm out to hurt her?"

"No, and stop being so defensive. My point is I don't think she ever really dealt with what happened in New York. She came to know the Lord, and her life has never been the same, but in my opinion she's never forgiven herself."

Carlos glanced about the barn. He'd detected a few things in their conversations. Those times he'd tried to get her to talk about herself, she'd turned the subject to another topic.

"What do you want me to do?" he asked.

His friend sighed. "Gain her trust and help her put it all behind her. A tall order, huh?"

Slowly the magnitude of Jack's request registered. Carlos forced a smile. "Right. For a brother, you don't ask much. Look, Jack, what I see in Cassidy is a beautiful young woman who loves the Lord. I've seen her in action at church, and she's awesome with people. I like her a lot. . .and I also know what you're talking about. She rarely talks about her feelings."

Jack leaned against the door to the tack room. "If you're

considering a relationship with her, just tread lightly. She's bound to run like a scared rabbit, and I don't want either of you hurt."

Carlos nodded. "Tonight, I want to talk to her about us. I'll pray for the right words and God's will."

"I can't ask for anything more."

❧

Carlos turned up the Tejano music pumping through his truck stereo and sang along in Spanish. He'd showered in record time, then changed into khakis and a green button-down shirt, his favorite. With the ends of his hair still damp, he'd rushed out the door only to dash back in for a squirt of aftershave.

In the truck, he once more contemplated Jack's words about Cassidy. Carlos couldn't decide whether his friend intended to give a viable warning or a cry for help. Probably both.

At times Carlos thought his attraction to Cassidy stemmed from their different personalities, more of a challenge to his ego than a special gift from God. He wished he could tell the difference; it might chart his course.

Carlos sighed. Her method of organization confused him. Other things took priority, and he didn't understand why. She spoke eagerly about fashions, but the affairs of the world soared beyond her view. Their ethnic differences didn't bother him, but Cassidy might have a problem with it. His mother certainly would.

At first he'd thought Cassidy couldn't possibly be a part of God's plan for his life, and he'd pushed her away until he couldn't stand it any longer. Sometimes he let his systematic way of processing information guide him rather than God.

I am absolutely losing my mind by allowing my emotions to take charge. Kissing Cassidy had to be one of the most stupid things he'd ever done. It went against all of his logic and reasoning. When he considered the time commitment involved in a relationship plus his career plans for the next

few years, he wanted to turn around and head back home.

Relationships were supposed to be a slow, gradual thing—weeks and months of developing a deep friendship and consulting God along the way.

"It's not supposed to happen too fast," he said aloud. God had to be in a relationship every step of the way or a couple had little chance to survive—if he and Cassidy were meant to survive.

He'd seen her love for the Lord every Sunday as she reached out to other members of the class. She didn't hesitate to offer impromptu prayers or to comfort others who had a problem. He'd seen her laugh and cry with them and willingly listen. Cassidy was a lovely little lady, but her heart surpassed her beauty.

He took another deep breath, and steered his truck into the circular driveway of Jack and Kristi's home. *Okay, Lord, this all scares me to death. Guide me on how I'm to proceed, whether it's to pursue Cassidy or abandon these feelings. I'm turning it all over to You—no matter how difficult.*

≈

Unlike their first dinner date, conversation flowed easily between Carlos and Cassidy. They laughed and teased each other, surprising Cassidy after she'd felt so uncomfortable with his kiss.

When the waiter brought their food, Carlos reached for her hand to ask the blessing. His touch affected her differently this time—soothing with a nuance of strength.

Once the waiter cleared their plates and they sat sipping after-dinner coffee, she found Carlos staring at her.

"Am I wearing chicken Alfredo on my chin?"

He shook his head. "No, I was thinking how much I enjoy your company."

"Thank you," she said, wondering if a smile had been permanently slapped across her face. "I like you, too."

He pushed away his cup and saucer. "To be blunt, I like

you very much." He hesitated, and her heart pounded while she waited for him to continue. "Do you want to see more of each other? To see if this is something God wants for us?" He rubbed his chin, reminding her of a psychology professor who used to analyze his students. "Am I pushing you on this? I know we've known each other for only two months—not a whole lot of time."

For the second time that evening, Cassidy groped for words. Her heart said one thing while her mind shouted another. One thing she knew for certain. "I want what God wants," she replied.

"So do I. I'd like to take things slow, for us to be the best of friends."

She nodded and swallowed a lump in her throat. Why did she feel like crying? "I'm a private person," she admitted. "I have a difficult time opening up, besides. . .we are so different."

He reached across the table and took her hand. "I think differences can be a blessing, if we use them to complement each other."

She laughed. "You have a more positive approach than I do. Your statement sounds like a well-versed politician."

"I'm practicing, but seriously it's all a little scary."

"A lot scary. You have plans for grad school and a future in politics. I have a business to run." Fear of the commitment involved coursed through her. "Maybe you've made a mistake."

He lifted a brow. "Do you want me to have made a mistake?"

Cassidy played the truth against what her mind dictated. She'd promised herself when she moved to Texas that God would be in control of her entire life—the present and the future. Holding on to her fears and not letting go of the past did not honor her trust in God.

"I have no idea how God can work this out, but I hope and pray it's not a mistake."

ten

As exhausted as Cassidy felt that night, she could not calm her mind and give in to sleep. Carlos's request to prayerfully consider the nature of their relationship left her nervous and frightened. All the logical reasons why she didn't want to acknowledge her growing feelings for him multiplied in the face of his interest in her. This would never work. They were at opposite ends of the spectrum, yet in her heart, she wanted it.

Skipping off to a fantasy world of happily-ever-after love with Carlos sounded like the old Cassidy—the one who easily gave up on the demands of life and eased into a make-believe existence. How easy it would be to let her commitment to Cassidy's Charm escape her and concentrate on this relationship. But everything she'd worked for, beginning at the rehabilitation center when she'd accepted Jesus Christ as her Lord and Savior, made such a move seem irresponsible. After all, Carlos admired the young woman who diligently sought to manage a boutique, not the drug-addicted teen who couldn't cope with life. Could she live up to his expectations when she had a hard enough time living up to her own?

For a little over four years, Jesus had been her constant companion. Now she yearned, yes, yearned, to venture a step further into a possible future with a wonderful man. Deep down she deliberated her worthiness of a godly man. Carlos must see something in her that she hadn't viewed in herself. Oh, she realized her capabilities and talents, especially when it came to people skills, a knack for business, and fashion merchandising. However, Carlos had a compelling need to make a difference in this world, and he was willing to pay

the price to achieve his goals. Those high aspirations made hers look like child's play.

Although the wolves from the past constantly nipped at her heels and reminded her of prior failures, Carlos hadn't asked her to give up anything. He merely wanted her to spread her wings and widen her heart.

The truth lay in her statement to Carlos: She wanted whatever God wanted.

Oh, Lord, help me rid my mind of the past. I know my family loves me as I am, and it's me who is holding on to my failures. Show me how to shake off those years when I didn't have You. If You desire Carlos and me to step forward with our hands firmly clasped in Yours, please tell us soon. And Lord, I'm afraid to open my heart and mind to him. I don't know how to tell him all those things that only You know. In Jesus' name, amen.

Days turned into weeks and the weeks into a month. Carlos called daily, often stopping by the boutique on his lunch hour. His position with the city demanded a great deal of his time, added to his already demanding schedule of working for Jack, leather-crafting, spending time with his mother, and completing the applications for grad school and scholarships. His schedule boggled her mind.

Carlos phoned the boutique one morning from his office. "I wanted to see you tonight, but I need to work on some financial-aid forms." He paused. "Of course, I want to see you every day."

"You're sweet, but you should work on the financial aid. I'm not going anywhere." She laughed lightly. "If you finish and want to call, fine. Although I might go to bed early and catch up on my sleep."

"Are you saying my girl needs her beauty rest?" he teased.

"Probably," she replied. "Your fast-paced life makes me tired thinking about it." She paused and absentmindedly leafed through her planner. "You know what? I have a Chamber of

Commerce meeting tonight. So now you can relax and get your work done."

"Will you call me when you get home?" he asked.

"I'll do better than that. I'll call on my cell phone while I drive back to Uncle Jack's."

The day sped by. Cassidy received a shipment from Dallas, and in between customers she checked through the new clothing, taking time to admire fabrics and styles. By mid-afternoon, she'd inventoried and priced the articles, which meant she could display them the following day.

Once she locked up for the night, she headed to the monthly business meeting, which included a catered dinner and discussion of the many items on the agenda. She'd attended these sessions every month since she'd opened Cassidy's Charm. They provided a way for her to meet area business people and to become involved in community affairs. Whether the Chamber elected to hold a fund-raiser or encouraged the community to bond together on an issue, Cassidy volunteered. She enjoyed helping and working with others. No one said a word about her young age, and the older business owners took her under their wing. One exception remained: Thelma Myers still managed to shun her.

As Cassidy entered the restaurant and took an assigned seat at one of the dining tables, she found herself seated beside Thelma. Definitely a disaster in the making, especially if she had any thoughts of enjoying her dinner and the meeting. In the past, this woman had insulted her at every opportunity and told her customers that Cassidy carried inferior merchandise. For her part, Cassidy refused to argue with the woman or enter into a debate about the quality of the boutique's clothing and accessories. She prayed for a softening of Mrs. Myers's heart and an opportunity to be a friend.

When Cassidy sat down at the table, she noticed the woman looked sullen, no doubt angry about the seating arrangement. Cassidy breathed a prayer and turned to speak to Thelma.

"I asked to change places with Margaret Winters, who owns the flower shop near your store," the older woman said, without glancing Cassidy's way.

"That's not necessary—"

"Oh, but it is. I have no desire to have my evening ruined by sitting next to you." She turned slightly to the left, as though Cassidy carried a lethal germ.

Cassidy felt her heart pound double time as she garnered the courage to attempt a civil conversation. "I wish we could be friends," she said softly. "You have your customers and I have mine. We don't have to be in competition with each other."

"Some of your customers used to be mine," Thelma snapped. "And you, *Child*, will never be a friend of mine."

Cassidy's face stung as if the woman had slapped her. Maybe the woman did need to find another spot at the table. In looking around, she saw the seats were full. A moment later, a minister prayed for God's blessings upon the meal and the business meeting to follow. Those in attendance began to eat, giving Thelma no choice but to endure Cassidy's company— or the other way around.

Cassidy loved Italian food, and the lasagna, fresh green salad, and hot rolls tempted her taste buds. Before she could begin, she made one more attempt at congeniality.

"I wish we could put our differences aside," she said, picking up her fork.

Thelma Myers whirled around, knocking Cassidy's plate and water upside down on her lap.

Cassidy felt the cold water saturate her clothing and heard the plop of lasagna as it slid off her napkin and attacked the delicate burnt-orange material of her skirt. Immediately, she scooted back from the table.

"My, my," Thelma said primly, placing her hand over her mouth. "What a pity, Dear. Looks like you won't be able to stay for tonight's meeting after all." She peered at the spreading red

stain. "And your outfit is probably ruined. Oh, well, with the price you pay for things, this must be a mere inconvenience."

The old Cassidy would have spread the food all over Thelma Myers's face, and the thought did cross her mind. But she didn't dare give in to those instincts.

The man beside her, the owner of a hardware store, must have heard Thelma's words, for he narrowed his gaze and drummed his fingers on the table. "How can I help you, Cassidy?" he asked, looking more uncomfortable than helpful.

She smiled at him and used her napkin to lift the plate and its contents back onto the table. "I have it," she replied as cheerfully as possible. If the ordeal hadn't made her so angry, she might have laughed. "Sure glad I don't have to give a speech tonight."

The man chuckled, his portly stomach shaking. "Don't know how many of us would have a sense of humor in a situation like this."

"Oh, this was an accident." She stared into Thelma's face. "Wasn't it, Mrs. Myers?"

The woman grabbed the seat of her chair and moved it away from Cassidy, scraping the floor in the process. "Don't get that mess on me," she said.

Cassidy bit her tongue before a terse reply escaped her lips. Instead, she prayed for patience and finished wiping the food from her skirt. She really had no choice but to leave the meeting. A few ladies left their seats to assist her, and one offered advice about removing the stain.

"Thank you so much," she said to them. "I think I need to go." Turning to the man beside her, she asked, "Can I stop by your store tomorrow and find out about tonight's meeting?"

"Of course," he said, dragging out his words. "Can I do anything else?"

Cassidy shook her head and stood. "I look like the beginnings of a laundry detergent commercial."

Everyone around her laughed except Thelma Myers; she

simply pulled her chair farther away from Cassidy.

I'm not contagious, Cassidy wanted to protest.

On her way home, before she picked up her cell phone to call Carlos, she prayed for Thelma Myers. Something had to be desperately wrong for anyone to deliberately live in such misery.

⁂

"*Mi hijo,* where have you been lately? You barely got here, and now it's time to leave," Carlos's mother said when he announced he needed to head home. They'd been sitting in her living room talking about the day.

"Mother, I'm working full time for the city, helping Jack, keeping up with the leather crafts, church work, working on scholarships for grad school, and I'm seeing somebody."

Her dark eyes twinkled, and she clasped her hands in a gesture of prayer. "Praise God. Who is she? José and Maria Lopez's daughter? Monica Rodriguez? Anita Garcia?"

He stared beyond her to capture the pictures of his brothers and sisters and their families. Taking a deep breath and sending a silent prayer, he studied his mother's face.

"No, Mother, she isn't any of those girls; it's Cassidy Frazier."

She paled. "Cassidy Frazier. What are you thinking?"

"Mother," Carlos began, realizing the war had begun.

"Your future," his mother's voice rose. "How can you help your people in the government when you choose a girl who is not Latino? Why would anyone vote for you? Think about what you're doing. You're. . .you're destroying your future." She fanned her face with the newspaper.

"Mother you're overreacting." He shook his head and fought the exasperation swelling inside him.

Her eyes blazed. "Not when this concerns the hope of the Latino people!"

Carlos wanted to laugh but thought better of it. He leaned forward and took her hand. "First of all, I'm not the hope of the Latino people. I'll leave that to Jesus. I'm one man who

believes God wants him in politics. Secondly, Cassidy and I are prayerfully seeking God's will as to what He desires of our relationship."

"You've talked to God about this girl?"

"Yes, Mother. I like her very much."

She shrugged her hand loose from his hold. "I haven't talked to God about her yet."

Carlos smiled. "I'd like for you to meet Cassidy. She's adorable, loveable—"

"Loveable? You use the word love with a girl whom you talk to God about but haven't introduced to your mother?" She dabbed at her eyes, but he didn't see any tears.

"When would you like to meet her?" he asked.

She sat straighter on the sofa and appeared to contemplate the matter. "Why not Friday night for dinner? I'll make something very nice for you and this. . .this girl."

"Cassidy Frazier is not just a 'girl' but a young woman," he repeated. "I don't believe we have plans for Friday, but I'll let you know tomorrow." He stood and gave her a smile. "I love you, Mother, but you can't have me with you forever."

His mother sniffed and patted her eyes again. "I know you have a life of your own, but you'll always be *mi hijo*. I will pray for you," she whispered.

He stifled a chuckle. "And I for you."

Once in his truck and en route to his apartment, he thought back over his mother's reaction to Cassidy. He didn't know whether to laugh or cry. His dear, sweet mother who believed she knew the best for her son.

Once she met Cassidy, he was positive she'd change her mind.

eleven

"Tell me about your mother," Cassidy said, flipping down the sun visor to catch a glimpse of her makeup in the mirror.

"She's rather short, like you, dark hair—"

"No, Carlos. I want to know about her personality, what she likes and doesn't like." Cassidy pulled on a stubborn lock of hair that refused to blend in with the others.

"Her favorite color is orange," he said with a smile tugging at his lips.

She couldn't help but laugh. Once he'd learned Thelma Myers had turned a plate of lasagna into Cassidy's lap and ruined her burnt-orange skirt, he'd made mention of it several times. His version made the incident sound comical, certainly a better thought than dwelling on the private war Cassidy was unwillingly involved in. She glanced down at her royal blue silk slacks and jacket. "This will have to do. Maybe she won't notice the color."

Carlos reached across the truck seat and grasped her hand. "You two will love each other, so don't worry about a thing. You look perfect."

She pushed the sun visor back into place and took a deep breath. "Thanks. I am a little anxious. Are there any topics I should avoid?"

He shook his head and squeezed her hand. "Just be yourself. My mom is a pretty good cook and loves to talk."

Cassidy swallowed hard and willed her frazzled nerves to calm. She'd met plenty of new people since coming to Brenham, but none of them were Carlos's mother.

Moments later, Carlos slowed his truck and pulled next to a small, white frame house sitting on about an acre of land.

Brightly colored impatiens circled two oak trees, and red hibiscus bloomed in an elongated flowerbed along with purple periwinkles and gold lantana. On the front porch, green ivy and purple passion hung from huge pots, all healthy and vibrant. Mexican heather bushes with their tiny purple flowers lined the outside of the porch, intermingled with dark green shrubs. The picturesque setting looked inviting and was obviously tended with care.

"This is lovely," Cassidy said. A woman who could grow such beautiful plants had to be a sweet lady.

A large, brown dog, displaying characteristics of several breeds, bounded up to the truck, wagging his tail. Carlos opened the door to pat the pet on the head.

"Hey, Rupert. How you doing, Fella?" The dog responded with an excited bark. "Got somebody I want you to meet." Carlos stepped around to open the truck door for Cassidy and properly introduced her to the dog. "He's a watch dog until he knows you," he told her, "then he's a pussycat."

Carlos and Cassidy walked hand in hand to the front door. Her stomach did a few mini flips. After all, this was *his* mother, and she'd found out from Kristi that Isabella Diaz ruled her family as a matriarch. True to Carlos's description, a short, attractive woman with traces of silver streaking through her hair, opened the door to greet them. Now Cassidy knew where he'd gotten his irresistible smile.

"Mother, this is Cassidy Frazier," Carlos said, not once letting go of Cassidy's hand. "Cassidy, this is my mother, Isabella Diaz."

"I've been looking forward to meeting you," Mrs. Diaz said, folding her hands in front of her. "Thank you for coming to dinner."

"You're welcome," Cassidy said, noting the elegant blue pantsuit the woman wore. "It's such a pleasure. Carlos has told me wonderful things about you," Cassidy replied.

Once Mrs. Diaz had ushered them into her living room,

Cassidy smelled something a little peculiar, not very appetizing. Carlos said his mother was a good cook; it must be some exotic dish whipped up especially for the evening. Cassidy relaxed a little, determined to enjoy herself and eat whatever his mother served.

❧

Carlos detected a strange smell the moment they entered the house, and suspicion shadowed his bright expectations for the evening. The longer the three sat in the living room, the more he realized his mother had planned a less-than-appetizing dinner.

He glanced about the homey little room with his mother's knick-knacks and tons of family pictures. She loved her children with a fierce, consuming passion. He should have realized she'd go to any length—or depth—to protect her youngest son from what she feared bordered on a terrible mistake. If he didn't love her so much, he would have been furious.

"Excuse me a moment," he said, rising to his feet. "I think I'll get a glass of water."

"I can do it for you, *mi hijo,*" his mother said, making an effort to still the rocking chair.

"I'm quite capable. You and Cassidy can visit, and I'll be right back." He turned to the women. "Would either of you like something?"

When they declined, he followed his nose toward the unsavory smell. Uneasiness mixed with queasiness churned about in his stomach. Surely she hadn't cooked tripe. Once in the kitchen, he saw the open windows and spotted the stew pot simmering on the gas stove. Beside the pot, he saw fresh corn tortillas, a bowl of chopped onion, and two lemons ready for slicing. Lifting the lid, he realized his worst fears. His mother had made *menudo*. His grandmother Diaz used to make the vile concoction, said it would cure anything. The smell alone would wake the dead. Whatever happened to fried chicken and mashed potatoes?

Lord, I need a little help here. Mother is trying to chase Cassidy away before she has a chance to prove herself. I know that You are the deciding factor in our relationship, but having Mother's blessing would make life a whole lot easier.

He poured a glass of water and walked back into the living room, where neither woman said a word. Tension as thick as the *menudo* settled about him.

"Mother, could I talk to you in the kitchen?" he asked, then took a long drink.

"Certainly," she replied, smoothing her hair.

In the privacy of the kitchen, Carlos did his best to form his words. "Mother, we have a problem here."

"And what is that?" she asked sweetly. Too sweetly.

He pointed to the stew pot. "What's cooking in here?"

"Why, *menudo*," she said without batting an eyelash.

He rested a hand on the counter. "You only cooked this stuff when Dad had been drinking and needed to sober up. Even then, the smell stayed in the house for days. No one would eat it, either. Why did you cook this for Cassidy?"

"I thought you'd want something authentic, something reflecting our culture," she replied, lifting her chin.

He knew her stubborn stance. How could he make sense of this without inviting an argument? "It looks to me as if you're trying to run Cassidy off."

"She's not right for you."

"You mean she isn't Latino," he said as gently as possible. "You're judging her on the basis of her skin color instead of who she is on the inside. How many times have we accused others of doing the same thing to us?"

She crossed her arms over her chest. "You make me sound prejudiced, when I'm only thinking of your future."

He expelled a heavy sigh. "My future is in God's hands. If you think Latinos will not vote for me someday because I *might* have an Anglo wife, then I don't need their votes. All I'm asking is for you to give her a chance. I want you to get to know her."

His mother refused to meet his gaze. "She talks funny."

"And you don't?"

She stiffened. "I'm proud of my heritage."

"And I'm sure she feels the same about hers."

His mother refused to look at him. "We need to have dinner," she said, breaking the silence.

"True, but not this." He pointed to the pot. "The vegetable soup you made a couple nights ago tasted great. Any left?"

She nodded, her gaze boring a hole in the refrigerator door. If she'd look at him, they could resolve this.

"Are there any tamales in the freezer?"

This time, her gaze lifted to his shirt. "Yes, your sisters and I made dozens last Saturday. But if she's used to yellow rice like the Mexican restaurants serve—"

"She will love your rice, the vegetable soup, the tamales, and your homemade corn tortillas," he replied, frustration beginning to take its toll. "I'll help you get it ready."

She shook her head, her arms still crossed. "I'm able to manage dinner. You keep your friend busy—show her old pictures of the family or take a walk outside."

"All right, but promise me you will give her a chance." He put his arms around her waist and peered into her rigid face.

"I will try," she said slowly, her sight level with his chin.

"Thank you," he replied. "Now what do you want me to do with the *menudo*? Give it to Rupert?"

She reached for her apron hanging on a chair. "Set the pot outside until I can do something with it. Rupert won't eat it."

Carlos would not comment. Someday this might be funny but not tonight. He shrugged off his irritation and headed toward the living room, believing no woman alive could be as stubborn as his mother.

ə∎

Curiosity pinched at Cassidy. What in the world had happened in the kitchen? And the smell? She'd seen a strange look on Carlos's face when he'd asked to speak with his mother

privately. Frankly, she felt a bit relieved. Isabella Diaz didn't seem friendly. She hadn't said a word or responded to Cassidy since Carlos had left the room for a glass of water. Possibly Mrs. Diaz was shy—or maybe not.

Cassidy folded her hands in her lap and studied every inch of the room while she waited for Carlos to return. While her parents' home barred no expense, containing the most exquisite art and European antiques available, Mrs. Diaz's furnishings were simple and comfortable. From the needlepoint pillows to the crocheted doilies positioned on the arms of an overstuffed chair, everything spoke of love and an appreciation for handicrafts.

Cassidy strained her ears. She could hear the hum of voices, but nothing audible. Her spirits sank. Why kid herself? Carlos's mother didn't like her.

Just when she'd decided she could no longer sit there alone, Carlos appeared in the doorway.

"Dinner will be a little late," he said, combing his fingers through his hair.

She studied him oddly. Mrs. Diaz had just said differently.

"Uh, when I went for the water, I saw it had burned."

Cassidy instantly regretted thinking Mrs. Diaz didn't want her there. "Oh, I'm so sorry. Let me help her. She shouldn't have to prepare dinner all over again." Glancing up at him, she caught his warm smile. "Let's take her out, Carlos. If she hadn't been talking with us, this wouldn't have happened."

"I think she'd feel uncomfortable if we offered dinner out," he said. "It shouldn't take too long for her to right things. In the meantime, she wants me to show you old family pictures or possibly take a walk."

"Okay," she replied dubiously. "I certainly wouldn't want to offend her."

Within thirty minutes, Mrs. Diaz called them to eat. The food tasted wonderful, and Cassidy complimented the woman. At first, Cassidy feared everything would taste spicy, but the

jalapenos were served on the side, making the food quite palatable.

Without a doubt, something had transpired between Carlos and his mother, an argument or a matter too personal to discuss in front of her. They both avoided looking at the other and were much too formal toward each other for a typical mother and son. Cassidy didn't need to deliberate the matter a moment longer; she understood the problem.

twelve

"You certainly are quiet," Carlos said, as he drove Cassidy home from his mother's house.

"I'm tired," she replied, stretching neck muscles.

"I think my mother upset you." He switched off the radio station and the sound of a lively Christian song faded to silence.

"She didn't say a thing, Carlos." She stared out at the window ahead. "We need to face the truth. I'm not what your mother wants for you. She wants a Latino, not a blue-eyed blond."

He sighed and reached across to take her hand. "How about what God wants? What you and I want?"

In the shadows, she turned her gaze to his. "I care too much to have your family ostracize you on account of me."

"They won't, believe me. Mother is simply unwilling to let go of her baby boy; she needs a little time." When Cassidy failed to comment, he added, "Has God told you we aren't supposed to be together?"

"No," she said, staring at the road ahead.

He pulled the truck off onto the grass. "Let's pray about this. God knows our hearts, and I hate the thought of you being upset."

She released her seat belt and slid over beside him. Gathering up her hands he prayed for guidance and a softening of his mother's heart.

Cassidy cried softly, and the sound of her weeping tugged at his heart. This mess with his mother had torn him apart, too. He'd seen Cassidy's compassion for others and how she gave of herself to so many people. In spending time together,

they'd visited sick church members, babysat Jack and Kristi's son, researched more about the John F. Kennedy School of Government, and cleaned out horse stalls. Every moment he spent with her confirmed his growing love. He had no idea how God planned to work out the months ahead while they explored each other's personalities, but he did know he didn't want to think of another day without her. One thing was certain: His organized, meticulous lifestyle had been tossed into the wind.

"Don't cry. God will work this out," he said, brushing her damp cheeks with his finger.

She leaned against his shoulder. "It's not just tonight, Carlos. I'm afraid I'm not good for you at all."

&

On Sunday morning during the music prelude, Cassidy reflected on Friday's dinner with Isabella Diaz. She couldn't put the matter out of her head. If she had been in the same situation as Mrs. Diaz, Cassidy might have reacted the same way. She'd always been a fighter when it came to standing up for her family or her faith, but holding on to Carlos sounded selfish. Had he forgotten her past? This godly man should have a woman with a pure legacy and a Latino background—not one who had experimented with drugs and lied to save her own skin. She shuddered, thinking about those months Uncle Jack spent in prison because of her.

Selfish, she repeated. Only a self-centered little girl would deliberately hold on to someone who deserved better. If she truly cared for him, she'd walk away and pray he'd find a suitable woman with the qualifications his mother held dear. Carlos must hear her whole story, and she needed to tell him soon.

As if hearing her doubts, Carlos reached for her hand, giving it a gentle squeeze. She glanced down at his tanned hand with his fingers wound around hers. When he spoke of his dreams and aspirations in making this country a better place to live, she

wanted to pray every minute of the day for God to honor his requests. How foolish of her to think she might one day share those triumphs. She trusted God for her life, and these doubts must be His way of pushing her to end the relationship.

Her family would be arriving on Tuesday evening to celebrate Thanksgiving with her. They planned to stay at the Davenport's B&B, and the turkey dinner would be there Thursday at noon. She couldn't wait to see her parents and Carly, show them her shop, and have them meet Carlos. She hated this indecision, this torment in her heart and mind about Carlos. The wavering made her feel fickle.

"I want to make sure you meet the rest of my family during the Thanksgiving week," Carlos whispered just then as the prelude continued. "With your parents coming in, I realize it will be hard arranging the time, but we can work out something."

She cringed at the thought of his brothers and sisters putting her through the same ordeal as his mother. "I can't," she whispered. "Besides, your mother hasn't invited me."

She felt his piercing stare and refused to glance his way. No one should impose where they aren't wanted, and his mother definitely didn't want her around. Cassidy refused to set foot in his mother's house and face her coldness. With her parents and sister in town, she should spend her time with family. Isabella Diaz and Thelma Myers ought to compare notes.

As the music concluded, Carlos leaned toward her once more. "This afternoon I want to talk. Too many things have been left unsaid that we need to straighten out."

She trembled. Maybe he'd realized the reality of their relationship and intended to end it today. His conclusion would make things so much easier. But why did she feel such dread?

Because I care about him. Because I don't want the relationship to end. Because I don't want to tell him about the

rest of the past and face his rejection. I want his family to like me. I want the impossible. Oh, God, am I asking too much? Am I once more being selfish?

After lunch, Carlos suggested saddling up the horses for a ride and Cassidy agreed. While she changed clothes, he talked to Jack.

"I'm going to talk to her about opening up to me," Carlos said, leading a mare from the stable. "I could use a prayer."

"You've got it. In fact, as soon as you leave, Kristi and I will pray together."

Riding across the fields a few minutes later with Cassidy, Carlos noted the cooler temperatures, and the crispness in the air reminded him of her attitude toward openness. He feared that if he broached the subject she might run, but it was a chance he had to take. They reined their horses toward the creek where they'd stopped weeks before.

"What do you think I want to talk about?" he asked.

"I don't know," she replied.

Frustration nibbled at him, but he refused to stop before he even got started. "Why is it you never tell me how you feel?"

"I do as long as it's not personal." The sharpness in her voice warned him he treaded on shaky ground.

"How are we ever going to get to know each other when you can't open up to me?"

"Are you wanting to quit?" She raised her chin and stiffened her position in the saddle.

"Not at all. I just want us to be open and honest."

"About what?"

A glimpse of her tense figure caused him to send a prayer skyward. "Why are you so insecure in our relationship, and why are you so willing to give up on us?"

Pain swept over her delicate features, and long moments passed before she spoke. "My past is disgusting—not just the condensed version but all of the things I did to those who loved me."

"Why don't you tell me about it?" He pulled the reins in on his mare. "In fact, we can walk if it makes things easier. Just understand none of what you have to say is going to make a difference with me."

She slid from the saddle as though she faced an executioner. For an instant, he wanted to spare her the heartache. They walked the horses, and he waited. The leaves rustled beneath their feet, the only sound breaking the silence. They tied their horses to a slender oak trunk, and he took her hand, cold and clammy.

At last she began. "You already know I had problems in high school with drugs. I want to tell you about it because it's important to me that you hear it all from my lips. Uncle Jack found out about my substance abuse and threatened to go to my dad. I got scared and told my dad he'd tried to assault me. As a result, Uncle Jack spent six months in jail for a crime he didn't commit. Then a friend of mine went to the police with the truth, and Jack was released. Of course, my dad didn't believe in his innocence and ran him off. That's how he ended up here in Texas."

"Baby, this isn't news to me. Jack told me the story long before I met you at the wedding—and you've told me before, too."

She wiped away a tear. "But I'm so ashamed. I didn't care what I did back then, not just to Uncle Jack but to my whole family and myself. I really don't think I had a conscience. I associated with the worst of scum, spread lies about my family, stole money from Mom and Dad, and stayed out all night just to hear them complain. My parents nearly divorced because of me, and I treated my younger sister, Carly, horribly. During Uncle Jack's trial, I faked tears and led the judge and jury to believe he was guilty." She caught her breath in sobs.

"Do you think any of your story affects how I feel about you?" he asked softly. "Are you not a child of God, a servant of the Lord Jesus Christ?"

"I understand I'm forgiven, but—"

"God has forgiven and forgotten your mistakes, and you need to do the same."

She continued to weep, and he wrapped his arms around her. "Let it go, Cassidy. The guilt is destroying the beautiful lady inside."

"I've tried," she managed, "and still it's there digging deeper. Sometimes at night, I'm physically sick. I feel as though my life in Christ is a dream, and I'll wake one morning to find I'm a despicable person again." She buried her face in his chest, and he cradled the back of her head in his hands. "Carlos, I can't possibly be good for you. What if we continue to see each other, and someday you're running for public office and your opponents find out?"

He chuckled lightly and stroked her hair, soft like a child's. "I have a brother who is serving time for robbing a convenience store," he said. "I think any political rival would have more of a field day with that information than a little teenage rebellion. Besides, it doesn't matter. The what-ifs in this world don't stand a chance as far as God's will is concerned."

"I want the best for you," she finally said. "I want to talk and act with your welfare in mind, not my own happiness."

"Then open up to me about everything, because I believe you are the very best for me."

She continued to cry softly against his chest. Every inch of him wanted her burden lifted and joy restored to her life.

"Can we pray about this?" he asked. "God doesn't want you to be miserable. He wants to take away the pain."

She nodded and his simple request for peace and healing in her life brought more tears. "There is no condemnation for those who are in Christ Jesus," he quoted from Romans after he finished praying. "Promise me you will repeat that verse every day until you are free from the guilt and shame."

She raised her tear-stained face and nodded. "I promise. Oh, Carlos, I don't deserve you."

"No," he replied. "I have the treasure." He pulled her against him, wanting desperately to do what only God promised. She felt tiny and fragile, like a delicate flower. He wanted to protect her from every evil of the world and shelter her from any unhappiness.

His gaze followed a red, yellow, and black form slithering not three feet in front of them.

"Baby," he said softly. "Remember the afternoon at the creek when I teased you about a snake?"

"Yes. You frightened me right out of the water."

"Don't move a muscle. This one is the real thing."

thirteen

She stiffened in his embrace. "What kind is it?"

"Oh," he whispered, "remember the little rhyme I taught you? This one is a perfect example."

Shaking uncontrollably, she remembered how to distinguish a coral snake. *Red and yellow kill a fellow, red and black friend of Jack.* The snake must be poisonous.

"It's crawling away," he said, his voice as calm as their surroundings. He held her quivering body firmly, all the while whispering tender words of comfort. "You can relax now," he said after several long moments. "Our friend has slipped off into the leaves."

She moistened her lips, still quivering. "Have. . .have you ever been bitten?"

"No. That's why you should always wear boots out here, and don't go sticking your hands in places where you can't see."

"I'll remember those words of wisdom," she said. "In fact, I'll never forget them."

Although she could step back from his embrace, she relished being held in his protective arms. The scent of his lightly spiced aftershave mixed with the woodsy aroma around them caressed her senses. Leaning into his chest, she allowed the delicious feeling of his arms around her to linger. Carlos always guarded his emotions toward her, avoiding compromising positions and tempting circumstances. He had a way of making her feel like a beautiful, treasured queen.

He lifted her chin with his finger and gently tasted her lips. In the past, she'd returned his gentle kisses with a certain shyness, but now she slipped her arms around his neck and invited more. What had happened to her desire to be innocent

and good in Carlos's eyes, just like those times when she worshiped God and temporarily forgot her sordid past? Perhaps her response to him stemmed from his urging to shove the past from her mind and heart, or the coral snake and its deadly threat. No matter, in his arms she felt secure and strangely reassured.

The kiss ended, and when she gazed into his dark eyes and saw the smoldering passion, it frightened her. Spellbound, she could only stare and drink in the realization of his love.

Her emotions swung from those of a giddy child to the feelings of a woman experiencing the desires of physical attraction. She sensed his passion heightening as his arms around her tightened. An alarm exploded in her head. This needed to stop now. She broke from his embrace.

"I'm sorry," he whispered. "I know better."

"It's my fault, too. I didn't try to stop you." She massaged her arms in an effort to control the trembling, not from the incident with the snake but from the danger of unbridled emotions. "Just because we're Christians doesn't mean we escape temptation," she said.

"Cassidy," he said, his words thick and labored. "I don't know what to say." He brushed back a wayward curl from her face and studied her as though searching for the proper words.

She touched her fingertips to his lips. "No need to say anything, except we're both frightened."

"My logical side says this is all happening too fast," he replied with a faint smile.

She nodded, while words fled her thoughts.

"I want to know everything about you," he said. "Your first words to your favorite professor in college. I want to hear your dreams and aspirations, everything."

The depth of his words caused her to shudder, but his request ushered in a deeper relationship. Normally she'd have abandoned a relationship by now, either out of boredom or because

of fear of involvement, but something within her refused to sever this tie. Was this selfishness or a gift from God?

"I'll try," she managed. "Pray for me; I've never done this before."

"Every moment of every day," he replied. A twist of wind whipped around the trees and wrapped the chill around them. "Let's get back to the horses."

"Good," she said. "I'm in the mood for a race."

He took her hand and squeezed it. "As long as you want to race horses rather than put distance between us."

"Already you know how I think," she said. "I can't run away, not this time."

⁂

Carlos picked up the phone and hesitated before punching in the familiar number for his mother's home. Ever since yesterday afternoon with Cassidy, he'd realized they'd bridged a gap in their relationship. She'd opened up to him—something Jack had viewed as nearly impossible—and promised to work harder at the fears that tormented her.

He shook his head. The coral snake had scared him, although he'd never admit it. But while Cassidy had trembled in his arms, he'd been reminded of the powers working in this world to keep people paralyzed with sin and guilt. How bright and colorful the temptations of this old earth.

He'd taken the time yesterday to inform Cassidy about the habits of coral snakes. They usually did not come around people, and if they did emerge from their secretive posts, they did so in the mornings.

"What do you do if a poisonous snake bites you?" she'd asked.

"First thing is to get to a hospital, but don't overdo it. If you get too excited, the venom can spread. If you are alone and walking, keep the bitten area still."

"What about those old cowboy movies where you lance the area and suck out the poison?"

He'd laughed. "Now the doctors say to leave it alone and not to apply a tourniquet either. In fact, don't use heat or ice or take any medicines. Simply get to a hospital."

"And how long do you have before it's too late?" she'd asked with a serious frown on her face.

"Very few people die of snake bites," he'd replied. "I think you watched too many old westerns. The trick is to get medical attention immediately."

She'd relaxed then. What a wonderful thought to always be able to calm her fears.

Turning his mind back to the present, Carlos waited for his mother to answer the phone. Each time he brought up the subject of Cassidy, she changed the topic. He'd never been one to act disrespectfully toward his parents, and he often kept his opinions to himself. But this situation was different: It dealt with a matter of the heart.

"Good to hear from you," his mother said. "Are you not coming by this afternoon?"

"Oh, yes, I'll be there. But I really need to talk to you now—about Cassidy."

"Why? You already know my feelings on the subject. She's not right for you."

Carlos allowed her words to settle before responding. "Mother, I care for Cassidy, and your biased opinion is driving a wedge between you and me. Is this what you really want for a mother and son? I don't believe either of us want hard feelings."

Silence reigned on the other end of the phone.

"No, Carlos, I do not," she said, her words laced with emotion. "You have never been serious about a girl before, and I expected. . .someone different."

"Cassidy might be the one God has selected for me. It's too early to know for sure, but I would appreciate your making an effort to get to know her."

Silence again, and as much as he wanted to jump in with

more of Cassidy's fine attributes, he closed his eyes and prayed for a bridging of the chasm separating him from his mother.

"All right. I'll try," she said in a small voice. "This is very hard for me."

He wondered if she intended for her weak tone to arouse sympathy, but he could not succumb to his mother's demands. "Thanks. All I can ask is an honest effort. Mom, I love you, but some things a man has to handle alone with God."

He hung up the phone and pictured his mother in her typical depressed mode, a pool of tears. He hated being the cause of her unhappiness, but he knew she'd change her mind once she spent time with Cassidy.

❧

On Tuesday, Cassidy flitted about the shop straightening displays and rearranging shelves. Luckily she didn't have many customers, because her mind wouldn't stay focused very long. Sometime late today her parents would arrive, and she wanted everything in the shop to be perfect. She hadn't seen them since last June, and for all of her declarations about being independent and self-reliant, she still missed Mom and Dad. And Carly, her dear, sweet little sister who always sent encouragement through E-mails and phone calls. Daily she sent a note of inspiration or forwarded a funny story.

Cassidy had poured out her heart about Carlos—the fears surrounding her growing love and the bubbling-over joy of simply being with him. She shared the funny moments, especially when her easy-going temperament met headlong with his perfectionism. Carly teased her relentlessly about the three of them having names that started with a C.

How amazing that her world could change so drastically in three short months. This could not all be a fantasy, but a blessing.

At noon, the boutique grew busy with local ladies snatching up shopping time during their lunch hour. Cassidy had allotted

a corner for holiday apparel in vivid reds, greens, and soft velvets ranging from separates to evening wear. Christmas sales climbed steadily, far more than she'd ever imagined.

While assisting a customer in putting together an outfit for her husband's office Christmas party, she heard a familiar voice echo across the room.

"Do you have anything in a size one for a little lady?" her father asked.

She whirled around to greet her parents and sister standing just inside the front door.

"Oh, Dad, you all look wonderful," she said, swallowing one tear after another. She'd never noticed how very much her father and uncle Jack were alike, not only in looks but also in mannerisms.

"You all look wonderful?" he mocked and turned to his wife and Carly. "Five months in Texas and she's already saying y'all."

"Miss, you'd better give those people a hug," the customer said, peering down at her over the top of a small pair of reading glasses.

Cassidy rushed into his outstretched arms and then hugged her mother and sister through a fog of tears. "I'm so glad to see you," she managed, laughing and crying at the same time.

"Cassidy, your boutique is really cool," Carly said, slowly making her way around the displays. "How do you keep from buying everything in your size?"

She laughed. "Extreme willpower, but you should see my closet at Uncle Jack and Kristi's. It's stuffed to the max."

"You do have lovely selections," her mother added, following Carly as though in a quest for the perfect find. "We're really proud of you."

Cassidy felt herself beam from the inside out. Every long moment, every irritating customer, and every day she couldn't wait to take off her shoes was worth the sound of those words.

"I think she got her business sense from me," her dad said, removing his jacket.

"And her fashion sense from me," her mother added, the scent of her expensive perfume following her through the store.

"And her love for clothes from me," Carly concluded. Her pale blue eyes searched the store. "The purses," she breathed, eyeing the many on display. "Are these the ones Carlos makes? I might have to buy another suitcase before we fly home on Sunday."

"Those are his, and I have more in the back," Cassidy replied, joining her sister.

"I want to see them all," Carly said, then whispered, "but most of all, I want to meet him. Unless you're afraid we'll run him off."

"I think he's made of stronger stuff," she said, with a teasing grin. "I might let you talk to him for a few minutes, if you mind your manners."

Her family browsed about the boutique while Cassidy waited on customers. Her dad sampled Irene's blueberry muffins and her mother sipped on the warm cappuccino while Carly fingered through the holiday clothing. Cassidy felt warm and fulfilled with her family's praise. The move to Brenham had been good for them all.

The bell over the door announced a visitor. Cassidy glanced up with a smile playing on her lips. She held her breath and felt her insides convulse. Isabella Diaz entered the shop with Thelma Myers right behind her.

fourteen

Cassidy inwardly cringed. All of the magnificent, delicious sensations of having her family visiting her instantly vanished.

"Good afternoon, Mrs. Diaz," she greeted and peeked around her to Thelma. "And you too, Mrs. Myers."

"Excuse me," Thelma said to Mrs. Diaz and briskly stepped in front of Carlos's mother. She eyed the others and pasted on a smile. "Cassidy dear, would you mind contributing to the city's fund for needy families? In purchasing Thanksgiving baskets, we ran short."

Cassidy walked toward Thelma and reached out to take her hand, but the woman quickly withdrew her grasp as though she feared soiling herself. Cassidy ignored the action and simply answered the question. "Yes, I'd be glad to help out. How much are the baskets?"

"Oh, you will?" A wave of surprise swept over the woman's face. She wore an excessive amount of makeup, which settled into the lines on her face. "The baskets are twenty-five dollars each, and that feeds a family of four with turkey, dressing, mashed potatoes, green bean casserole, rolls, and pumpkin pie."

"Okay, let me write you a check." Cassidy turned to Mrs. Diaz. "I'll be with you in one minute."

While writing out the check, she took a quick glimpse of Mrs. Diaz, who seemed to be studying her closely. Cassidy smiled, all the while wondering what had prompted her visit and hoping Thelma Myers didn't make a scene. *That's all I need—to have Thelma start in with her barbs in front of Carlos's mother and my family.*

She handed a folded check to the woman, who instantly

opened it. Her eyes widened then narrowed as she stuck the piece of paper inside an envelope.

"No doubt you are doing well by selling inferior products to the helpless ladies in this community," she said within earshot of Mrs. Diaz. Her searing stare pierced Cassidy. "Your shop is bigger than mine; I look forward to running you out of business and taking this one off your hands."

Mrs. Diaz gasped, and Cassidy felt her face warm with the insult. She took a deep breath and straightened her five-foot frame.

"Mrs. Myers, I don't know why you dislike me so, but this I will say. You have been rude and said nasty things about me to other business owners in the community. As a result, you are the one who looks bad. I will continue to run my boutique to the best of my ability and pray God softens your heart." She summoned enough stamina to continue. "I'd still like to be friends."

With a whisk of her skirt, Thelma Myers whirled around and left the shop, leaving a trail of pity in her wake.

"I'm so sorry," Mrs. Diaz said barely above a whisper. "Does she always say such terrible things to you?"

Cassidy nodded and nibbled at her lip. "She has since I opened. As I told her, all I can do is pray."

Mrs. Diaz reached for her hand and patted it with the other. "She's jealous because you have a beautiful shop. I've been standing here looking at the clothes and other things you have here, and you have every right to be proud."

She relaxed with the woman's gentle hold of her hand. "Thank you. God has blessed me far more than I deserve."

Mrs. Diaz smiled and Cassidy captured her rich brown gaze so much like Carlos's eyes.

"I came here to apologize for last week," Mrs. Diaz said, "and ask if we could be friends."

"Of course," Cassidy replied, relief and surprise replacing the tension remaining from Thelma's unpleasantness. "I

would love getting to know you better."

The woman smiled again, rather nervously but nevertheless genuinely. "Carlos told me last night that your family is coming for Thanksgiving." When Cassidy nodded she continued, "Perhaps Thanksgiving night, if your family permits, you might join Carlos at our home. All of my children and grandchildren will be there, and I'd like for you to meet them."

"I'd love to come," Cassidy said. "I'm sure something can be worked out." With Mrs. Diaz still clinging to her hand, Cassidy swung her attention to her family.

"Mom, Dad, Carly, I'd like for you to meet Mrs. Diaz, Carlos's mother."

૨૦

The hours before Thanksgiving were filled with laughter and reminiscing about childhood days. Carly spent Tuesday and Wednesday night with Cassidy while their parents stayed at Country Charm Bed and Breakfast. Carly and Cassidy couldn't stop talking to each other, and Cassidy wondered why so much time had to pass before she discovered how much she adored her little sister. Carly wanted to know everything about Carlos, even to the number of times he'd kissed her.

"I don't have a clue," Cassidy replied while they talked in the darkness of their room on Tuesday night. Positioned in twin beds, she thought they resembled teens sharing secrets. "I didn't count."

"Yes, you have; you just don't want to tell me."

"Why do you want to know?" Cassidy asked, her sides aching from laughing.

"More juicy stuff to talk about to my sorority sisters," Carly said. "My life is boring, and yours sounds exciting."

"Wrong again," Cassidy replied. "I work, and I go to church, and I see Carlos."

"Isn't God good?" her sister asked. "I love what He's doing in your life."

Cassidy turned her head toward the faint outline of her

sister's tiny frame. "Thanks, Sis, and yes, I agree."

During the traditional feast on Thursday, her father told the story of how he'd come to Texas four years earlier to reconcile differences with Jack and had met up with Kristi's fierce temper. He'd overheard her planning to let the air out of his tires so he couldn't meet up with his brother. Then Uncle Jack recalled how Kristi had thrown a rug out the back door of the bed and breakfast and sent him sprawling to the ground. She'd thought she hurt him, and when she'd dashed out of the house to check, she'd caught her heel in the sidewalk and broken her foot. Poor Kristi; they picked on her for an hour, but she took the teasing in stride, laughing with them.

Cassidy adored Paula and Rick Davenport, Kristi's parents. Paula, a tall, attractive redhead, and Rick, a typical white-haired cowboy type, had prepared the dinner together, from the crisp veggie tray to the assortment of pies. The couple thrived on hosting guests at their bed and breakfast and served them generous helpings of Southern hospitality and Christian love.

Amid the festivities and love surrounding her, Cassidy missed Carlos, although she understood he needed to be with his family and she needed to be with hers. He planned to arrive at the B&B around five o'clock to meet her family before whisking her off to his mother's home. The thought of introductions to his family made her squirm. She stared down at her pale arm. All the suntan lotion in the world would not make her Latino, neither would it change her eye color. She inwardly smiled. Something must have happened to change Mrs. Diaz's mind on Tuesday for her to apologize and issue a Thanksgiving invitation. The woman had made a distinct effort to be gracious, and Cassidy hoped that effort was sincere.

After several board games and during the second quarter of a football game, Carlos arrived. Cassidy felt shy. God had put this wonderful man in her life, and she felt proud and blessed at the same time.

"Carlos and I met a few years back," her dad said, reaching out to shake the younger man's hand. "I appreciated your friendship with Jack then, and now I'm glad you're looking out for my little girl."

"Me, too," her mother said. "I'm Lena Frazier. I've heard nothing but good things about you."

Carly made them all laugh. "Cassidy said you were good looking, but she didn't say *that* good looking."

Once on their way to his mom's house, Carlos reached across the seat of his truck and gave Cassidy's hand a squeeze. "You have a great family."

"Thanks. I really felt nervous with you meeting them and all."

"Not any more nervous than I feel about you meeting mine."

She shot a surprised glance his way. "Why? I'm the outsider horning in on their territory."

He laughed. "You're beginning to sound like a Texan."

She shrugged. "I have the whole collection of John Wayne westerns."

He roared. "You amaze me; so do I. Western movies are the last thing I thought we'd have in common."

"God does have a sense of humor," she said. "Which one is your favorite?"

"Hmm, not sure. Probably all the ones about Texas."

She laughed. "Better get yourself an exact opinion before you head into politics. You don't want to get labeled before you get started."

Once the truck pulled into his mother's driveway, apprehension trickled through Cassidy's body. One evening with Mrs. Diaz had been bad enough, but what would she do with a whole family of unfriendly people? She knew enough Spanish from college to understand the language, but when people spoke fast, she got lost. "Does your family talk to each other in Spanish or English?"

"Both, but you'll be just fine," Carlos said as if reading her thoughts. "They are going to love you like. . .pumpkin pie and whipped cream."

From the moment his mother opened the door, Carlos's family opened their arms to her. He had two sisters: Marta and Yolanda, who had two children each. Cassidy met Ruberto and his wife with their three children, and Hector and his wife and their two children. When they all held hands in prayer, Cassidy learned Pepe was the brother in prison. Each family member petitioned God to change their brother's heart.

She discovered how Carlos received his training with kids. She watched him change diapers, spoon-feed a baby who had a better liking for vegetables than Walker, and play with the older ones. His nieces and nephews clamored for his attention, and when she joined in on the fun, they warmed to her, too. By the time she and Carlos left, they had invitations to visit the rest of his family well into the New Year.

That night Cassidy lay awake with Carly in the bed beside her. What an absolutely perfect Thanksgiving, and she had so much for which to be thankful. Her parents eagerly voiced their approval of Carlos, and his family had been wonderful. Tonight, as they'd said their good-byes, Mrs. Diaz had kissed her on the cheek. What a sweet blessing. If only. . .she could rid her mind of the guilt. She'd been praying, but her past still sickened her. She wept softly so as not to wake her sister.

Quietly she crept from the bed and knelt on the floor. *Lord God, please take away these haunting memories. I know I won't ever forget what happened, but I need to feel clean. Sometimes I think it's good to remember the past, so I can stand humble in light of Your grace. But this dirty, horrible feeling isn't right, and I don't know how to get rid of it. Please help me, Lord, amen.*

"Cassidy, are you all right?" Carly whispered. She slipped from her bed and joined her.

"Oh, I'm fine," Cassidy replied.

Her sister hugged her shoulders. "Nightmares?"

"Something like that." She leaned her head on her sister as the tears continued to stream down her cheeks.

"I have a good ear."

Cassidy shook her head in an effort to dispel the agony. "I'd give anything not to have done those terrible things to you, Mom and Dad and Uncle Jack. God has forgiven me, but I can't forget."

"Honey, it's been over four years. This thing will eat you alive if you don't let God take it away."

"Pray for me, will you? Every time I think of my family, I want to crawl into a hole, and I'm afraid it will ruin my relationship with Carlos. Most of the time, I feel so worthless."

"I love you, Cassidy. Of course I'll pray."

fifteen

During the month of December, Cassidy wore a sweater only three times, and then she roasted. She kept shorts and T-shirts from the summer stacked in her drawers and regularly donned them after work. Kristi promised her cold days in January, but Cassidy didn't believe Brenham ever felt the real cold that she'd known back home. She seriously considered shipping her winter clothes back to Carly. They were so close in size, she knew the clothes would fit—and they'd certainly get more use.

She and Carlos spent their spare time planning a Christmas party for their Sunday school class, shopping for special gifts, and even baking Mexican chocolate sticks. The treats emerged from the oven hot and tantalizingly sweet, but a try at cutout sugar cookies was an unmitigated disaster.

"They won't lift off the wax paper," Cassidy wailed. "Look at them, Carlos. Every star looks deformed, and I haven't been able to sprinkle the colored sugar on any of them."

He glanced over her shoulder. "Did you dip the cookie cutter in flour?"

"Yes." She tilted her head, and he planted a kiss on her cheek. "I think the dough is too soft."

"Possibly." He yanked on a roll of paper towels and wiped the tip of her nose. "Flour," he said with a grin.

She snapped her fingers. "Yes, flour. It needs more flour."

While she dumped in more of the white powdery stuff, Carlos read the recipe for the third time.

"Honey," he began, pointing to the cookbook. "It says here, we're supposed to refrigerate the dough so it rolls out easier."

Cassidy cringed and accidentally tilted the bag of flour,

releasing a mound of it into the bowl. "What am I going to do with this mess? Every inch of Kristi's kitchen is covered in white, and now I've ruined our masterpiece."

He laughed while his gaze trailed over the kitchen. "Tell you what, Miss Chef. Let's throw away this cookie dough, clean up, and head into town for one of those refrigerated dough packages you slice, bake, and decorate."

"Wonderful," she exclaimed and turned to give him her best smile. She toyed with the sides of his dark hair with her fingertips.

"Are you putting flour in my hair?" he asked.

"Yes, Mr. Diaz, I am. I want to see how you'll look when you're older."

He wrapped his arms around her waist and pulled her tighter. "I hope you're there to see it," he whispered.

She felt a shiver twist up her spine.

"Did I scare you?" he asked.

Cassidy nibbled at her lip. "Just a little."

He brushed a kiss against her lips. "Me, too, but I like the sound of it." He held her a moment longer, but Kristi walked in.

"I thought you two were baking cookies," she said, peering over the white-dusted counter.

"We are," Cassidy replied. "The dough is resting."

Kristi shook her head. "You might have better luck buying the refrigerated kind."

Carlos laughed. "My thoughts exactly."

As the countdown before Christmas inched closer, Cassidy struggled with what to get Carlos for Christmas. Cologne sounded too normal and expected—and her Carlos was not a normal kind of guy. Clothing seemed too personal, and by no means did she intend to purchase him an engraved pen-and-pencil set. He already had a good watch. Then she remembered him eyeing a little electronic gadget when shopping in Austin. The perfect gift for the organized, perfectionist type of man.

Carlos swung his chair away from his computer and headed to the kitchen for a glass of water. He couldn't concentrate on his scholarship applications when he hadn't decided on the ideal gift for Cassidy. His lack of funds put a damper on the really great things, and Jack and Kristi hadn't helped at all. He'd run the gamut of perfume, jewelry, and even a uniquely designed jacket, but nothing fit the zany little blond who had stolen his heart. To make matters worse, her parents wanted her to fly home on the Saturday evening before Christmas, giving them Sunday, Monday, and Christmas Day with their daughter. No last-minute shopping for him; he had three days to make his purchase.

On Friday night, December 21, he escorted Cassidy to a Houston restaurant Jack had recommended. Carlos had downloaded the directions from his computer, but as he and Cassidy drove through the Galleria area, he realized the street numbers didn't match up with his online map. Surely this minor setback didn't foreshadow her reaction to his gift. After two wrong turns, he finally settled them into the designated steak-and-seafood restaurant with her Christmas present in his pocket.

As they shared a multi-layer chocolate cake filled with a pudding-like pecan sauce, more thick, rich chocolate, a topping of cherries, and a huge dollop of whipped cream, he took the plunge. "I brought your gift."

"Um, so did I," she replied, setting her fork beside the plate. She dabbed her mouth with a linen napkin and reached for her purse. "I have to give you mine first because I can't wait any longer, and if you don't like it, I can return it for something else." She sighed. "Please, tell me if you don't like the gift, because you won't hurt my feelings at all."

He caught himself in a perpetual smile. Sparkling rays of light from the candle between them danced off her hair like spun gold, and her cheeks flushed in the excitement. Gazing

into her eyes, the color of a deep blue sky before a tempest, he wanted to suspend the moment, storing it in his memory to replay on days that were hurried and weary.

"Whatever you give me, I will like because it came from you," he said, realizing he could easily reveal the growing love filling his heart.

She returned his smile shyly and handed him a small package. No matter if her gift was a bottle of the worst smelling aftershave, he intended to make a huge fuss.

Carlos untied the red ribbon and lifted the box from its gold foil paper, slowly and deliberately calculating her anticipation. He read the box; surely she had not purchased this paragon of an organized man's dream. Lifting the cardboard flap, he pulled out a personal digital assistant. He didn't know what to say.

"Is it okay?" she asked hesitantly, crossing her arms on the table. "I remember you looking at them when we were shopping."

Carlos glanced up into her cherubic face. "This is perfect—too much for you to spend. I'm pleased, very pleased." He pulled out the directions and glanced at them quickly. "This is perfect," he repeated and carefully folded the paper. Slipping it inside, he reached across the table for her hand. "Thank you so much. It will be put to good use—on a daily basis—just wait and see."

She beamed, and he wondered if any Christmas lights could compare to the light in his Cassidy's eyes. Yes, his Cassidy. Reaching into his sports coat pocket, he retrieved his gift for her. The same anxiousness he'd seen in her now enveloped him.

She took the square package and shook it lightly, then untied the gold ribbon and eased open the ends of the deep green paper. Before her lay a navy blue velvet box, and she offered him another smile. Gingerly she lifted the lid and her eyes widened.

"Oh, Carlos. You knew how much I needed a watch. This is beautiful." She held it up to the candlelight before slipping it over her wrist.

"There's an inscription on the back," he said. . .and waited.

Cassidy turned the watch over in her hand. "Esther 4:14," she said. "For such a time as this." Her eyes moistened. "I will treasure this always."

He took the watch and placed it around her tiny wrist. "I had them shorten the band. Hopefully it fits." When the delicate band rested easily against her skin, he released a breath he hadn't realized he was holding.

She wiggled her wrist, allowing the candlelight to illuminate the small gold ringlets encircling her wrist. "Thank you. Merry Christmas. Now whenever I check the time, I'll think of you."

"My point," he said, holding onto her small fingers. "I don't want you to forget me."

The silent reply shining from her eyes told him fathoms about her feelings. Whatever had he done before Cassidy graced his life? Whatever would he do without her?

The future looked unclear with so many uncertainties surrounding his education. He believed God had called him into politics, but of course those aspirations could change. He didn't expect to earn a decent income for a long time. Six months ago, budgeting for two ranked at the bottom of his list of priorities, but his life had taken a strange twist. How could he support a wife—Cassidy—who had never been deprived of anything?

Sacrifices had been part of his life from the time he was a little boy living with an alcoholic father. Meals at his house consisted of beans, rice, and occasionally chicken. They shopped for clothes at secondhand shops, and his mother worked long hours cleaning houses. All of his brothers and sisters found jobs as soon as someone would hire them. Except Pepe. While the rest of the Diaz siblings found the Lord, Pepe decided to take what he didn't have. In the midst

of Pepe's rebellion, their father contracted cirrhosis. But during his last days he'd surrendered his life to the Lord.

Not exactly a storybook life, but reality in full force. His family had the Lord and a strong mother to instill good morals, but Carlos's siblings were the lucky ones—except Pepe. Too often he'd seen the results of poverty and illiteracy lead to destruction of human lives and souls. This was his focus, his life calling. People needed the Lord foremost in their lives, but they also needed education and an opportunity to become productive citizens through dedicated leaders.

He'd told Cassidy all this one Sunday afternoon. She'd applauded his commitment to the Latino people and all those who suffered under devastating conditions, but she hadn't lived his lifestyle and couldn't understand the level of depression they faced. She had sympathy; he had empathy.

Only the weeks and months ahead would reveal God's plan for their lives. He wanted to leave it alone—not fret over it, but his personality yearned for control. Leaving things in God's hands sounded easier than actually doing it.

❧

Carlos and Cassidy spent New Year's Eve chaperoning a lock-in for the church's high school students at their fellowship center. They helped gather up enough food, drinks, games, prizes, top hats, horns, and popular Christian CDs for an army of party-going teens. During the day, Carlos had enlisted a few of his buddies to blow up nearly six hundred balloons. Of course, he had to feed them for payment.

That night they held lip-sync contests and gave away movie and bowling passes, and the pastor spoke about beginning the New Year with Christ. A couple of students made decisions for the Lord, which led to another round of celebrating.

The hours sped by faster than Carlos had anticipated. When his watch alerted him that it was ten minutes before midnight, he searched for Cassidy and found her talking to a group of freshman girls. They were all laughing about one of

the other chaperone's rendition of an old Beach Boys tune.

"Excuse me," he began, "can I borrow Cassidy for a few minutes?"

"You mean, until it's midnight so you can kiss her," one freckle-faced girl said. "I think the rules state hugging but no kissing."

The other girls giggled, but he was prepared for their teasing. "Oh, no, I have to put her to work."

"Doing what?" another asked.

He managed his best innocent look. "Blowing up the rest of the balloons. She forgot a few and time's running out."

All six girls glanced at the ceiling and the net teetering back and forth. "Naw," the freckled girl replied.

"You're right," he said and shook his head. "Truthfully she needs to call her parents in New York and wish them a happy New Year."

The girls swallowed his story, which held a lot of truth, and Cassidy rose from the floor to follow him.

"Carlos, it's past midnight in New York," she said, frowning. "You shouldn't have lied to those girls."

"No, I didn't. Call them real quick back in the kitchen before midnight. You can use my cell phone."

She lifted a brow as he handed her the phone. "I see what you're up to." She punched in her parents' number, but the answering machine picked up. "Hi, Mom, Dad, and Carly. Happy New Year from Texas."

She handed him back the phone just as the kids began the final countdown in the other room. Carlos grabbed her by the hand and pulled her away from the doorway.

As the shouts of zero echoed and the hoots and hollers roared, he gathered her up into his arms and kissed her soundly. Her lips were feather-soft, cold, and tasted like cola.

"Happy New Year," he said. "Can't think of anything better than a New Year's kiss from the prettiest lady here. I won the prize."

·······Presents·······

Great Inspirational Romance at a Great Price!

Heartsong Presents books are inspirational romances in contemporary and historical settings, designed to give you an enjoyable, spirit-lifting reading experience. You can choose wonderfully written titles from some of today's best authors like Hannah Alexander, Irene B. Brand, Yvonne Lehman, Tracie Peterson, and many others.

When ordering quantities less than twelve, above titles are $2.95 each.
Not all titles may be available at time of order.